CATH HOWE

Not
MY
Fault

To Judith, Ella and Miranda
C. H.

First published 2019 by Nosy Crow Ltd
The Crow's Nest, 14 Baden Place
Crosby Row, London SE1 1YW
www.nosycrow.com

ISBN: 978 1 78800 2 868

A CIP catalogue record for this book is available from the
British Library.

Printed and bound in Great Britain by Clays Ltd, Elcograf S.p.A.
Typeset by Tiger Media.

Papers used by Nosy Crow are made from wood grown in
sustainable forests.

3 5 7 9 10 8 6 4

Rose:
The Extra
Push

I am Rose Elisabeth Sheridan and I am the one to blame.

I am with Maya on the roundabout again.

Maya shouts, "I'm a Frisbee. Spin me!"

Dad waves to me and goes off to get the newspaper.

The ancient roundabout, like a flaky wooden plate, has curved metal bars to grip. Its top edge rears up. Its bottom edge has dug a sort of sandy trench.

It's always Maya's turn.

My sister lies face down, splayed like a star, her toes scudding the ground.

I push off. *Wheeeeeee.*

"Harder!" she calls.

I look up at the sky, and I run alongside while she soars around the top.

My arms ache. Another heave.

"Harder!"

The plate rotates her down again.

I'll show you!

"Ooooaaargh!" she goes, just as I force my arms to push again and leap on.

An animal noise; a squeal.

The roundabout judders.

I tumble off, staring over at my sister.

Maya lies bent like a strange puppet with her leg trapped underneath her body.

I am Rose Elisabeth Sheridan.

I can still hear Maya's scream inside my head.

I can still feel the judder.

In the hushed family room in the hospital, while we wait for news of Maya's operation, I hear Dad whisper to Mum, "I saw Rose give that roundabout an extra push. Why would she do that?"

Even after all the horrid operations and hospital treatments to help fix Maya's leg, it will always be my fault.

And, of course, my sister stopped talking to me and started hating me instead.

Maya:
Egg Art

You say my name like 'FIRE', 'Maya'. If you said it wrong, that would be a different person.

"So … big day, you two!" Gran came rushing in to say goodbye and began wandering around our kitchen, moving things.

Dad was on his laptop, half pulling on his jacket. Busy.

Mum was on her phone, nibbling toast. *Tap tap tap*. Busy, busy.

Gran grabbed me from behind in a hot hug that smelled of oil paints.

"What's up, Scamp? Eat up!"

I smiled for her.

Then I glared at the boiled egg, all pale with its head off and its insides dribbling down my blue bug egg cup. "I already ate my toast. I can't eat this egg, Gran. It's too wibbly."

Why did Mum make us eat boiled eggs on important days? Why couldn't we have cereal like normal people? I pushed the evil egg away.

Mum looked up. "Just get on with your breakfast, Maya, or we'll be late. Don't make a performance out of it."

Gran dried a pan. "I always find eggs cook

5

best if you time them for exactly four and a half minutes."

Mum stopped tapping on her phone. "I *did* time them for four and a half minutes. There's nothing wrong with her egg." She sighed. "Was yours all right, Rose? Did you eat it?"

Of course Goody-Goody Rose had eaten her egg. She was by the sink rinsing her plate right now before putting it in the dishwasher, her long blonde hair falling over her eyes. "Yes, Mum," she murmured, pointing first one long beautiful bare foot then the other.

"And you're both all packed?" Gran asked. "Got your wellies ... raincoats? They can't guarantee the weather, you know. It is a lovely area, though." She waved the air with her tea towel. "We went camping to that bit of Wales once and Grandad was chased by some cows. They can be very aggressive."

I grinned at Gran. "Did they catch him?"

"No," she said. "He managed to drag himself over a fence. Couldn't speak for three minutes."

"Mum got me some new boots, Gran," Rose said, all *smarm smarm*.

I sighed. "I've been packed for years. Mum

made us tick off everything on the whole list."

"You've only just had the summer holidays," Gran said. "I think you're incredibly lucky going away again."

I pulled out my phone and texted Georgie.

Are you at school yet?

Mum frowned at her phone. "Rose, I've just had an email from the Tumblers. Looks like the Regionals are going to clash with our trip to Spain at Easter."

Dad groaned. "I've already booked that off as holiday."

"Well, apparently, the Regionals are now scheduled to be in the school holiday. Compulsory. Looks like we'll have to switch to May half-term."

"That might suit me better actually," Dad said, typing and nodding.

My head shot up. "Er, no," I said. "We can't go away then. It's my half-term drama camp."

The kitchen went quiet. Dad did a wary look. "Well now…" he said.

"Damn," said Mum. "I knew there was something." Then she turned to my sister. "I suppose it's because the squad have only just accepted you, Rose. That's why we didn't know the date." Mum scrolled through the message again. "I suppose these gymnastics events are set months in advance."

"I … I think those are the only dates … for squad events." Sweet and helpful Rose was now emptying the cutlery from the top of the dishwasher. "I think there's a visiting team from Germany. So I have to be available. I mean, Clemmy said—"

"Have we paid for Maya's drama thing?" Mum asked Dad.

Dad shrugged. "We put her name on a list. But we haven't paid yet."

My heart filled up with black spirals like a raging monster twisting inside its cavern at the bottom of the sea. My voice was giant. "You *said* I could go. And why do you keep calling it a *drama thing*? It's not a *thing*. It's a proper … like educational and real learning… Everyone's going. I said yes. You agreed."

Mum stood up. "Stop shouting!"

"I didn't shout!"

"Listen to yourself!"

"You're shouting too!"

Gran's arms gathered me up. "Look … if Maya's

set her heart on the drama..." She pulled me close. "Is this an actual play, love? I used to love acting."

Tears pricked behind my eyes.

"Yes. You could come and watch, with Grandad." Gran felt warm. I hugged her fiercely. "Unless Mum and Dad ruin it. The rest of us can still go on holiday over Easter like we planned. Rose could stay with Clemmy. She practically lives there anyway."

Mum rammed her phone back in her bag. "There'll be other drama camps. I will not discuss our holiday with you yelling at us." She crossed the kitchen and put her plate in the dishwasher. "This yelling you do these days is completely *not on*! Now finish that egg."

"But..."

"That's enough!" Dad said. "You heard your mother."

"If Grandad and I can be any help...?" Gran patted my shoulder.

"You can't help!" I sobbed.

Mum looked at Dad.

Angry tears ran down my cheeks. I rubbed them away. "Th-th-thanks, Gran."

My phone beeped. Georgie.

At school now.

"You won't be allowed your phone on School Journey," Rose murmured.

I stared at her.

Mum nodded. "Rose is right; they said that at the meeting. No phones."

Mum and Dad disappeared out into the hall.

Gran bent down by the dishwasher, sliding in plates, *clack clack*.

Rose stretched a long elegant hand and flicked back her hair, her chin tilted up. She looked so stupid standing there.

I wished I could make storms like Greek gods do – stretch out my fingers, but with thunder and lightning crackling up through me, the whole kitchen filling with a massive deluge, washing the world away, leaving me on my own in the middle of a wild sea.

Why did Rose always get what *she* wanted? Why was everything always easy for *her*?

Cupped in my fingers, the egg was quite heavy. My hand felt tingly.

Rose's eyes met mine. She tensed.

I threw the egg; Rose leaped. *Thwack!* Wet

shell spattered on the wall beside the dishwasher.

Missed.

My brown comet had been good, though, soaring across the kitchen... *Whee!*

"What was that?" Gran turned and stared at the white transparent stuff, clinging ... dribbling...

"I slipped," I said. "My egg sort of ... flew off."

A picture flashed into my mind of my sister perfectly poised on a narrow bar, flipping a cartwheel, while crowds and crowds of people cheered around her.

Rose is perfect, you see, and I would never be. She made sure of that.

Rose:
Kadunking

Maya, you are such a liar!

I felt my face flush red.

"How odd," Gran said, staring at Maya, then at me and then at Maya again.

I bit the inside of my mouth, felt a sharp stab of pain, bit again...

I wish I could throw you at the wall.

No, I don't.

I watched egg goo dribble down. Gran got a cloth and wiped it.

"Time to go, you two!" Mum called.

I stared into Maya's eyes.

Just leave me alone.

"Are you all right, Rose, love?" Gran asked.

"Yes, Gran," I said.

But inside I was falling. Like that egg.

✗

Mum and me had to walk behind Maya up the road; of course she wouldn't walk with us. My suitcase *kadunked* and Mum talked.

My sister – if she wasn't happy, everyone had to know. My friend Clemmy could do her exact voice: "It's not fair!" with a big whine like 'fe-yur'. She filled up the whole room, the whole house, the whole planet. Poor Mum! She always did so much to help Maya and she was just a brat in return.

At school we sat on opposite sides of the class, but I could hear Maya's loud laugh every day, like a headache.

It started to rain. Mum kept suggesting things I might have forgotten, but I don't think she really thought I had.

"How about your hat?"

"It's in my case."

"The binoculars from Grandad?"

"Yes, Mum."

Our eyes drifted up the road to watch my sister.

I hate watching the limp – her bad leg is stiffer than her other one. No wonder when her ankle has eleven bits of metal all doing different jobs.

A person walking past might not notice her jerky wobble. But I always see it. Even though she isn't slow, she can't run; she isn't allowed to.

"So, what an exciting trip," Mum went on. "Are all your friends looking forward to it?"

"Um…"

I'm not like Maya; I don't exactly have loads of friends.

Stevie was a sort of friend; I sat next to her in maths and we used to make up doodles of little aliens with long arms. But Stevie was always with Pip the rest of the time. I liked Nicole, but she got fed up when I kept saying I didn't have time to go to her house because of gym. Clemmy said Nicole was jealous because she would never be selected for the squad if she tried out for it.

The rain got harder. I did my coat up.

"She'll get soaked," Mum muttered. Her voice rose to a yell. "Maya, where's your coat?"

My sister didn't turn round.

"PUT YOUR COAT ON!"

"I don't know where it is!" Maya called over her shoulder.

"Honestly, *that girl*!" Mum sped up to catch her and grabbed Maya's suitcase handle.

Maya just walked off, leaving Mum undoing the zip and burrowing around in the case.

Rain was coming down fast now, running down my nose. I caught up just as Mum pulled Maya's raincoat out. We watched Maya disappear round the top of the road.

"Maya! Maya!" Mum screeched, like a massive emergency.

We rushed after my sister, Mum pulling Maya's case and me pulling mine – up to the top, round the corner, and into Brooklands Avenue.

"Stop!" Mum called.

Maya was actually speeding up. We passed the bus stop and there was the school entrance, with lots of parents and children milling about.

"Maya Sheridan!" Mum yelled, rushing into the crowd. "Come back here!"

I felt red flush up my cheeks as people turned to stare. Everyone must have noticed.

"Hi, Rose!" someone's mum said. "Is everything all right?"

I tried to remember whose mum she was. "Y-yes," I said.

I stood with the cases, watching all the happy people saying goodbye. Other people's families looked so friendly and normal compared to us.

Clemmy came bursting out of the crowd. "Rose!" She wore her white pompom hat and sparkly earrings, like a party person. She grabbed my arm and I let go of Maya's case. It rolled over on its side. "Why have you brought two suitcases? Have you seen the email about Regionals? Are you excited? I am soooo excited I am literally going to burst. School Journey is going to be epic." Clemmy frowned. "Well, say something."

Maya:
The New
Horrible Teacher

Mum came elbowing through the crowd. "Maya! You are not leaving in this rude way!"

But I was.

I ignored Mum's red, angry face. Some people turned to stare so I stared back. I slung the stupid raincoat over my shoulders and went under the canopy by the school office.

My friend Archie clutched his lunchbox tightly across his chest. It was orange with a picture of a galactic star ship. "Hi, Maya!"

"Did your mum drop you off already?" I asked.

"Yep," said Archie, then softly, "I've got *everything*." His eyes darted to left and right. "Will it still be raining when we get to Wales?"

"Dunno…" I said.

Archie is a friendly kind of person but today he seemed … different.

Mum gripped my arm. "Maya. You haven't even said goodbye."

"Bye," I said, all flat, staring at a dripping corner of the canopy. Mum pulled me into a hug that wasn't nice because she held me too hard. "Have a lovely time," she said, as if having a lovely time was a grim prison thing. I wriggled away.

She still wouldn't go. "Maya, if you get any

pain…"

"I'm not talking about it."

"But you won't do anything silly? Just take it gently. I've discussed your leg with Mr Goodman and Mrs Olson is a trained nurse…"

"Just go!" I said.

Mum bit her lip. Her smile came on. "Did your mum drop you off, Archie?"

"I already asked him that," I said.

"I'm allowed to ask him too," Mum snapped.

Archie fiddled with his lunchbox.

Mum stalked away to hug Rose. Sometimes when people kiss they bang noses. When Mum and me hug our arms don't go to the right places; one of us steps too close or too far away. But when Mum hugged Rose, long and slow, it looked like an advert for something so nice that everyone would want to buy it. They were talking now: Mum still holding Rose round the shoulders, not wanting to let her go.

"What ya got for lunch, Archie?" I asked.

Archie whipped his lunchbox behind him. "Not telling."

Why was everything horrid today?

I went and got my case, which was lying

abandoned on its side. My friend Georgie waved and rushed over. "So, did you bring slippers? I wasn't going to but then I changed my mind."

"Listen," I said, "Mum says they are going to cancel my drama just so Rose can do her gym competition. She is wrecking my life!"

"That is soooo unfair! Oh, Maya!" Georgie grabbed me in a hug and her long dark hair flapped against my cheeks. "I looked for you and I couldn't see you and here you are and Dillon and me have already signed in our cases so do yours quickly then we can all get on the coach," she said all in one breath. "Did you bring something for the Talent Show on the last evening?"

We spun each other round.

My friends Dillon and Jake came over and we all jumped up and down and sang "We are going to Whitesands!!" like vibrating snakes, with Dillon going "*Bootshka ki bootshka*". Everyone grinned so we did it again louder.

Dillon waved to his mum and his little brother. "See ya Friday. Don't miss me too much!"

"We won't," his brother shouted.

"And don't play on my Xbox!"

His brother giggled and we all laughed.

"Where's Archie?" Jake asked.

"He's in a mood," I said.

Four teachers were coming with us. I knew three of them: Mr Goodman, our class teacher; Miss Stewart, and Mrs Olson, a helper sort of teacher.

But there was another person standing by the coach with a clipboard, making everyone line up and checking off their cases. She was older than the other teachers, in folds of skirts covered in red and purple flowers, like curtains. Her hair was a tight ball behind her head fixed with a big metal clip.

I nudged Georgie. "Who's that?"

"She's called Miss Bruce," she said.

Miss Bruce beckoned to us. "Lunchboxes will go on the rack when you get on. Plastic bags are bad for the environment." She reached into Jake's carrier bag and pulled out three bags of jelly snakes and two packets of chocolate stars. Jake's face fell.

"Jake, you big banana," I whispered. "Why didn't you hide them?"

Miss Bruce waved a rubbish bag. "Food is provided on this trip."

All Jake could say was, "Yes, Miss. OK, Miss."

She watched while he dropped everything in.

"Blimey," Dillon said. "She's checking everything. Where are your sweets, Maya?"

"Bottom of my case," I murmured.

Miss Bruce moved out into the crowd. The megaphone popped and crackled and her small voice turned into a very loud one. "Right, parents, don't drag it out; just say goodbye. Take home any mobile phones; we won't be needing those. The children just need to check in their cases sensibly."

Jake made a face of agony. "Is *she* really coming with us?"

Rose:
A Hug That
Wasn't a Hug

Clemmy nudged me. "Are you listening, Rose?"

I nodded.

The school car park was full of parents under umbrellas. Mum was chatting to another parent now. Clemmy had just begun describing how to build towards a backflip using a washing rack and a kitchen stool. But all I could think of was how Mum had just said goodbye to me.

"I'm so proud of you. Our sensible Rosie!"

I'd been picturing just running back home for the week with only Maya going. I could be in my room. The house would be quiet.

But then Mum stopped hugging me and held me at arm's length, staring into my face. "Rose, love, I know you and Maya won't be together much on School Journey… The thing is, Maya's been a bit wild recently. We just need you to … look out for her."

Her hands were heavy on my shoulders.

"Just in a friendly way. If she's doing an activity, or in an evening … it's just keeping your eyes and ears open. She won't even notice." Mum sighed. "Please, Rose, just keep an eye on her?"

Sad feelings choked me. "But we'll be in different groups."

"Of course, but it would be easy just to … pop your head round the door." Mum smoothed some hair behind my ear. "Anyway, have a great trip, love."

I gulped. Spying on Maya.

Memories from more than a year ago filled my mind. I couldn't stop them:

Maya leaping up on the old roundabout, calling, "I'm a Frisbee, spin me!"

Dad calling to me. "Just going to get a newspaper. Won't be a minute."

Jumping on, pushing hard off the ground. The roundabout lurching into life, wheezing and clanking. Maya, lying with arms wide like a star, her toes scudding the sandy ground, shouting, "Do it! Do it again!"

Clemmy's voice was loud by my ear. "Are you listening *at all*?"

"I was … am listening," I said. "I was just thinking about my sister."

"Don't waste your time on her," Clemmy said. "We won't be with her anyway. Tell yourself she's on the moon."

If only you were on the moon, Maya. If only I could push a button and send you there.

My mind jolted. I must be such a horrible person. I flushed.

Clemmy was still staring at me, her head on one side.

"I … I… My mum asked me to keep an eye on Maya."

"Keep an eye on *her*! Oh, Rose!" Clemmy shook her head. "Your problem is you're too nice. Parents always ask those sorts of things."

"Do they?"

"Yes and anyway keeping an eye on us is what teachers are for."

My tongue found the place inside my cheek where I'd been biting. My teeth clenched round the bump I'd made there.

I can't stop watching you, can I, Maya? Mum doesn't need to ask.

Maya:
A Big Flowery Blob

I nudged Dillon. "Let's grab the back seats for the journey."

"We'll have to be quick," he said. "Everyone will want to sit there."

"What about Archie?" Jake said.

"There isn't time," I said. "Come on."

"I'll keep a place for him," Jake said.

Our class teacher Mr Goodman was waiting by the coach door in the navy tracksuit that he wore for PE lessons. He grinned from under his wild curly hair. "Hi, Georgie, Jake, Maya, Dillon. All set and ready to roll?"

"You *are* coming with us, aren't you, Mr Goodman?" Georgie asked.

"You bet! And Miss Bruce has agreed to come on the trip at very short notice because Mr Edwards isn't well. She used to work here. And Mrs Olson will deal with any medical issues. I'm just checking for absentees and then we'll be on our way." He nodded to a parent. "Don't worry, we'll let families know we got there in one piece."

Georgie hopped up and down and did a sweet smile. "Can we get on the coach now, Mr Goodman?"

"Is your case on board, Georgie? Well, I suppose…"

"Quick!" shouted Jake and Dillon. Now it was a race down the bus. We fell on to the long back seat, pushing and bumping places.

"I'm next to Dillon!" I shouted.

"Ow, you trod on my toe!" called Jake.

Something changed in the air, making us all look up. "*What* do you children think you are doing?"

A big flowery blob with a cross voice blocking all the light. Miss Bruce.

The giggles fizzled out. "Who gave you permission to leap on and rush to the back like a bunch of SAVAGES?"

My eyes dropped down to her feet. Big black boots, like a soldier would wear. They made me burst into laughter all over again. Jake and Georgie and Dillon were all quiet and my laughs turned into little choking spurts and then coughs.

"Please, Miss, Mr Goodman said we could get on." Jake sounded sensible and good.

Miss Bruce sort of puffed up bigger. "I was behind him, young man, and he did not even get a chance to open his mouth before you four sprang up the steps."

I felt another laugh coming and squashed it to a snort.

"Well, you can all get straight *off* again."

"Yes, Miss."

"Yes, Miss Bruce."

As soon as I got down the steps Rose's friend Clemmy appeared beside me. "You're out of control, Maya," she said, snide and gloaty. "I'm surprised the teachers let you come on School Journey at all."

I stuck out my tongue.

Clemmy stalked away, back to my sister.

"Listening please," blasted Miss Bruce through the megaphone, nearly making me deaf because I was right beside her.

All the people for miles went quiet.

"Children on the coach, please. Except for Jake, Georgie, Dillon and Maya. You four will wait until last. The rest of you, say goodbye NOW."

We had to watch everyone else leap on. Then Ollie Palmer waved at us from the back seat. Rage twisted inside me. So unfair!

Archie came up to me, still clutching his lunchbox.

I rolled my eyes.

"Where have you been?" Dillon asked him.

"Nowhere," he said and he just walked away to the coach.

Now it was just the four of us and a crowd of waving parents. Miss Bruce said, "OK, Georgie, Jake, Dillon, slot in wherever there's a space. Maya, wait here."

My mouth burst open. "But…"

"I don't like buts."

I fumed, watching Dillon sprint away up the steps.

Jake shrugged. "See you on the bus, Maya."

Georgie bit her lip, turned, and ran after them.

And I was left there with horrid Miss Bruce and her lists.

Mr Goodman came out of the school office. "Maya, we've decided you're going to sit with Bonnie on the way to Whitesands."

What? Bonnie wasn't my friend. She always sat with a special extra teacher.

Now I saw her waving to the school secretary and being led over from the office by Miss Stewart. She must be staying for six weeks from the size of her suitcase. She had a sparkly purple jacket on with the hood up. She beamed at me, a smile that grew bigger and bigger with every step.

I stared at the teachers, outraged.

"If you argue, Maya, you will sit next to me instead," said Miss Bruce.

Rose:
A Present

"I've got something for you," Gran had said a few days ago.

I had called in on my way back from school. Grandad was in the garden. Gran was working on her deer picture, still trying to get the greens right. She pushed up the sleeves on the old man's shirt that she wore as an overall. She always has crusty paint all the way up her wrists in lots of colours.

We stood together to look at her painting. She was using oil paints. She always says her pictures are never finished. First, Gran had sketched the deer outdoors in the park. He was in the middle of a big clump of trees and he was just turning so the sun lit up his antlers like fire. All her sketches were pinned up round the edges of the easel. "For inspiration and so I get the legs right," she said.

She handed me a small parcel wrapped in shiny paper. "I thought you might need this."

I unwrapped the most beautiful sketchbook, small with a blue cover, just the right size for my rucksack.

"One condition." Gran's eyes twinkled. "I get to see the sketches when you come home."

"I love it," I said.

"It is a holiday, Rose, love," Grandad said,

appearing in the doorway, rubbing his hands together, dusty from the garden. "Enjoy yourself."

Maya:
Bonnie

The window ran with rain.

I sat seething, half buried by a massive pink sparkly bag that poked into my leg.

"Do you like my emergency handbag?" Bonnie asked.

My perfect sister got to sit with her friend, but I was stuck with Bonnie. I couldn't even see where Georgie was, or talk to her, for the whole entire journey.

The coach pulled out of the car park and the school faded to a speck behind us. Mr Goodman started to tell us all about Whitesands and all the activities we would be doing.

I hadn't waved to Mum. She probably hadn't waited.

I sneaked a look behind me. Rose and Clemmy Pantock-Reid were two seats behind on the other side of the aisle. Clemmy caught my eye and pursed her lips together. *Keep staring but you won't win. You are a worm*, her eyes said.

Everything that had happened just now seemed to join up: Clemmy saying "You're out of control", and me being stuck with Bonnie. I bet Clemmy and Rose pointed me and my friends out to Miss Bruce when we ran to get the back seat. Maybe Rose even told Miss Bruce about me throwing the egg at breakfast just to get me in trouble?

So now Miss Bruce thought I was a bad person.

Rose and me never talked to each other. Even though we lived in the same house and we were in the same class at school.

My sister was too perfect to be with me.

Bonnie wasn't actually that bad. I'd never spoken to her properly before. She had a friend called Lola, but Lola wasn't allowed to come on the trip. Miss Stewart, Bonnie's special teacher, came down the coach to say hello. Dad said Miss Stewart looked about sixteen. She had red boots on and a scarf made of lots of different-coloured bits of material tied together.

"Isn't this exciting?"

I pulled faces out of the window.

Bonnie asked, "What are you doing?"

So I made a really stretched mouth and started waggling my ears at a man in a van with a picture of bread and butter on the side that said *Naturally Good!*

Bonnie copied me, squashing her nose into a flat piggy shape and goggling her eyes. But then she turned and made the same face at Mr Goodman who was looking back across the aisle.

He shook his head at her. "That's not very nice!" He smiled. "Are you excited, Bonnie? We've all been building up to this trip, haven't we? And hopefully when the rain clears up we'll have some lovely weather." I listened to Mr Goodman telling Bonnie all about how to keep safe on the trip and how she had to stay with Miss Stewart who had come specially.

The coach was speeding along now. I hated sitting all the time. My legs wanted to kick out. I kicked the seats in front and Bonnie joined in. Pip stuck her face through the gap. "Stop kicking our seats."

Bonnie and me giggled.

"I'm not," I said, because that time it was Bonnie.

At least I wasn't sitting with my sister. Rose did all the main things in life before me, like walking and talking, but that's only because Rose got here first. Mum had Rose in September, then eleven months later, the next August, she had me. I'm not as tall and my hands are chunky, like Dad's. Mum and Rose have long fingers. I did learn to ride my bike only one week after Rose, though, when I was three. Gran says I just kept trying again and again until I got it.

I watched the blurry wet windows and followed a raindrop down with my finger. This time yesterday I had been on my own in the house, apart from Tiggy from next door, our rubbish babysitter. She was on the phone to her boyfriend. Tiggy is always on the phone to her boyfriend. And, of course, Rose was out being brilliant.

Standing in the doorway of Rose's bedroom, I always breathe the sweet smell – Freesia Fling. Gran gave us both little bottles at Christmas but my one was Amber Nights – a strong dark sort of smell. Like polish, Dad said. It gave him a headache.

No Entry read a sign on Rose's door. So in I went.

Rose's books are all lined up alphabetically, all sticking out the same amount, the framed photos all fanned out on the chest of drawers, the trophies gleaming on the shelf. If Rose had been the one who had the accident, all these would be mine. Awarded to Rose Sheridan. People used to drink out of these kinds of goblets in the court of King Arthur. Once I took one downstairs and filled it with lemonade, but it tasted of dust.

I sprayed freesia behind each ear.

I pulled off the lid of the washing basket and looked inside. Just clothes.

The bed? I launched myself across the duvet and probed around in the pyjamas. Nothing.

The toy hammock over the bed? I yanked out the biggest bear from the bottom and tossed him over my shoulder into the bin. It rained animals.

Then I saw the old gym bag poking out from behind her dressing gown and a rectangular shape at the bottom. Ha! I thrust my hand inside and pulled out Rose's diary – purple leather, page a day, *MY DIARY* in gold on the front.

I leafed through. Gym things … names of movements … wish lists … paper cuts and origami that Rose had made. A flower cut from a magazine. School Journey packing list tucked into the pages. *Notes, slippers, one cuddly toy, sketching things, mini binoculars from Grandad, beach shoes.*

Don't forget your new boots, I wrote with a smiley face. *Watch out, there's a Maya about.*

I strolled back to my room. And there they all

were on my door – this week's Post-it notes from Rose for my collection.

STAY IN YOUR OWN ROOM.

I KNOW YOU'VE BEEN IN AGAIN.

LEAVE MY THINGS ALONE, MAYA SHERIDAN.

Rose:
Clemmy on
the Bus

"We'd better get organised, Rose," Clemmy said by my ear.

Fields flicked by. The coach was full of chatting. It had stopped raining. I'd checked the weather forecast for Wales with Grandad and it wasn't supposed to rain all week.

I pulled my green and blue striped rucksack on to my knees – it was one of the gym competition ones; the whole squad got given one. The Tumblers logo is a person doing a backflip and the two halves of the body nearly joining together. So clever. I'd been practising drawing it.

I rummaged around for my new sketchbook.

"I've made us a training schedule," Clemmy said.

"Oh…" I flicked through the blank pages. I love white pages in a new notebook, the feeling of all the things you might draw. As if the pages have invisible drawings and you just have to find them.

"We might be … too busy," I said.

I had written a list of the activities we could do at Whitesands Centre. The place had been open for more than ten years. Mr Goodman said it was perfectly safe and the instructors looked really friendly on the website. I was quite interested in the Sensory Trail because you had to feel your way.

There were film clips and I'd watched all of them.

"We should get up early every day and do extra runs and fitness. You really need to practise, Rose."

Clemmy knew so much about training because of her mum being the main coach at our club. She wanted to help me be the best I could be gymnastically. That was what we always shouted at the end of training. "Be the best you can be, gymnasticalleee!"

It was just I had brought three books to read in case I woke up early. And I had been looking forward to making my trip diary with sketches and things.

"It's only five days…" I murmured.

Clemmy tutted. "Don't be lazy, Rose."

"Sorry," I said.

I found myself thinking about home. Coming back home after gym was always like a silent war. No wonder I spent more and more time with Clemmy. I had only started going to Clemmy's gym club a year ago for somewhere to be while Maya had all her physio sessions. It was much more fun than sitting in the hospital with Mum. Then Clemmy said I should do competitions and try for the squad.

Clemmy rolled her head down on to her chest. "And … breathe," she said.

I copied. It was just like having a personal trainer.

I peeped over at Maya. She was waving her arms around, making Bonnie laugh.

You never sit still, Maya. No wonder you smashed Dad's glasses. And those disgusting faces you're always making when we're having tea, like animals or someone being sick. No wonder Dad says, "Get down. Just go if you are going to ruin the atmosphere."

"Do you think they'll give us scores for the activities?" Clemmy asked in an odd breathing-out voice.

"They might not want to."

"Like in school when the teachers say we're all winners. I mean, that's just a lie," Clemmy said.

I pushed my sketchbook back in my bag.

Clemmy pulled on my arm. "Did you notice when we got on the bus that Archie Bates was up to something?"

I sighed. "No. Is he?"

"Honestly, Rose, you never notice *anything*!"

I peeped at Maya again. That used to be me laughing with her, before the accident. We used to laugh so much.

Maya:
Archie's
Lunchtime
Secret

Long journeys are *so* boring!

At last we stopped for lunch in a park. We all flopped down on the grass and Miss Bruce told us where to sit and where the bins were, as if we were blind, and said, "Stay where I can see you."

"I am *starving*," Jake said.

We compared packed lunches.

Rose walked past with Clemmy and they whispered something to each other, clung together and strutted away.

Archie hadn't come over to sit with us, even though he always did at school. He was on his own under a tree.

I finished my sandwich and went to see him. "Why are you on your own?"

He looked up at me warily. "I like it."

"Why aren't you eating your lunch? Did you finish it?"

"Yes."

"That's not true. I watched you. You haven't been eating at all. What's in your lunchbox?"

"Nothing!" he said, hugging the box as if it was the Crown Jewels.

His box was bashed about. Holes had been punched in the side. Something was sticking out of the back.

I sat down beside him. "What are you planning?" I whispered, like a detective.

Archie's eyes darted to check no one was watching. "Turn round."

We turned. He leaned in. "You have to not tell anyone, Maya."

"Of course I won't. What's wrong? Did someone hurt your lunch?"

"No." He eased open the catch on the box. "It's not sandwiches or sweets in here…" A brown whiskery nose peeped out and then disappeared again. "It's Nibble."

His hamster! His busy little face was like a miracle.

A big rush of excitement shot through me. "You brought Nibble on School Journey! Can I stroke him?"

"No!" He shut the catch.

"Go on."

"It's too risky. Someone'll see."

Archie's face closed up and he sat there just stroking the box.

"So why did you bring him then?"

"I had to. Last time I went away to my gran's

49

my brother forgot to look after him and he died."

"That's terrible!"

We both thought for a minute.

"This one's Nibble Two," Archie said. "I've brought everything he needs."

Normally Archie was a funny, light sort of person. He ran his hand over the puncture marks. "Air holes," he said.

He showed me the water bottle pushed in the hole round the back. "I'll take him out whenever I can."

"But won't your family notice he's gone?"

"They'll forget." He sighed. "They always forget."

"But what about all the activities, like when you have to climb something?"

"I'll hide him."

I grinned. I turned and checked that the teachers were still busy having their lunches near the coach. All my class were still chatting.

"I can help look after him," I said. "I love hamsters. Can we tell Georgie, Jake and Dillon?"

Archie frowned and glanced across to where our lot were sitting. Bonnie sat near the others, showing Miss Stewart all the things in her pink handbag.

He nodded. "Not Bonnie, though. She'd tell everyone."

Archie was right. Bonnie would be too excited.

I got up. "Hey, what about your lunch?"

"I brought a sandwich in my pocket."

I sent the others over to see him one at a time. Jake came back doing pretend tongue-zipping. Dillon came back saying, "Well, it's up to him. I won't say anything to anyone." Georgie came back, really excited and pulled me close. "Oh, Maya, poor Archie. No wonder he's been different, and we all thought he was just in a bad mood and how are we going to stop the teachers from finding out and they mustn't? Maya, we have to help him! Will he need extra hamster food?"

"He's brought it," I said.

"I haven't got a hamster, but I have got a cat."

Clemmy walked past to put her rubbish in a bin, Rose trailing along beside her. "What's wrong with Archie? Is he sick? Or just sick of you, Maya Sheridan?"

"None of your business," I snapped.

"So why are you all whispering?"

"Go away. Leave us alone. We don't want to talk to you," I said.

Rose pulled on Clemmy's arm. But Clemmy scowled. "Wouldn't stay here anyway. You're bound to fall into some sort of mess."

"You'd better watch you don't fall in it with me then," I said.

"You're not normal," she jeered, walking away.

I waited for the exact right moment, then called, "Who wants to be normal if it means being like you, Clemmy Pants All Peed?"

All around me my class erupted into laughs.

Clemmy wheeled round. "It's Pantock-Reid!"

"That's what I said."

"No, you did not!"

✗

On the coach again, and there were high hedges on either side, like walls, closing around us. We sat behind a caravan for miles. The air got hot and smelly: a mixture of sweets and whiffy trainers. I had to get out soon or I would choke to death.

We were playing Spot the Yellow Car and Bonnie kept calling out, "Over there ... there's one ... another one!" She was good at finding them. I pointed to a sheep in a field, looking back at me with that blank face sheep have. I put on a new sheep voice: "Baaa. You humans in your metal box whizzing past me. I've got nothing to worry about except how much grass I can eat."

We both made sheep noises and then it was just Bonnie being a sheep cos it was making my throat hurt.

Pip's head poked round from the seats in front. "Why are you two so annoying?"

I shrugged. I couldn't speak cos I was a sheep.

I made up a song about Rose and I found out Bonnie was a really good singer and also that she would go on singing a song really loudly even when the teachers said to stop.

"Daisy, Daisy give me your answer do.

Rose's head flew off, she found it down the loo…"

I checked Nosy Rose out of the corner of my eye. Her neck and cheeks were flaming red.

The teachers even had to get out of their seats to come and tell Bonnie to stop. Hilarious!

Rose:
Seeing the
Sea

I love when you go on holiday and the first time you see the sea. It's just this blue strip that's a bit darker than the sky and you think you imagined it and then you get surer and surer. Mr Goodman said the first person to see the sea would get a team point and Jason Daniels at the front kept shouting that he could see it even when we were all surrounded by hedges and nowhere near. The roads got straighter and there were rusty brown hills, and green and lime and old potato colours.

Whitesands Centre was right beside the sea down a driveway. We all piled off the coach. We were told our cabin numbers. Mine was Cabin Three.

We jumped off the coach and then Miss Bruce said, "Find your cabin and make your bed. Meet us by the cafeteria at four thirty. What time did I say?"

"Four thirty," we all chanted.

And then we were FREE.

We dragged our cases out. We spun.

"I can smell the sea!" I said.

"I can see it … and an island … and a beach. Look!" Clemmy said.

We rushed to find our cabin and get sorted out. All the cabins had window boxes with bright flowers like Swiss chalets. We were going to be sharing with

Willow, Tasha, Stevie and Pip. Clemmy said we should have the bunks nearest the door so we could do extra training, and the others didn't seem to mind. Some things had to stay in my case because the cupboards weren't big enough for six people. I went outside on the steps and looked down at the sparkling sea and the wide beach. Behind me, everyone was calling in the cabins and running around exploring.

Before the accident we always used to go on family holidays to the sea – wandering on the sand, collecting shells, climbing on the rocks.

You and me used to build dams of stones to make new channels for the sea, didn't we, Maya? But the sea always found a way round them.

I quickly got used to the smell: a bit of PE changing rooms and a bit of forests.

I had the top bunk. We made our beds.

Clemmy checked the bathroom and found a spider's web up in the corner. "I wish I had my phone," she said. "The shower looks gross! Dad would have written to the school to get some money back."

Maya:
Coloured
Sprinkles

They showed us around the whole place. Whitesands had loads of activities and even its own shop. There was a garden in the middle with a big circle of grass and wooden houses where everyone could sit with their friends, called The Hang-Out.

"This would be ideal for our extra morning exercise," I heard Clemmy say to Rose.

"You have to ask a teacher," Rose replied.

"Fine by me," Miss Stewart said. "I'm always up early. I'll take you down there."

Because Rose and Clemmy were real proper athletes; they couldn't just do what everyone else does, could they? I mean, it's called a 'hang-out', but of course they couldn't just *hang out* in it!

We were all seriously starving by the time we ate. Nobody said you couldn't have chips with garlic bread, so I did. I also had brownies, cauliflower, yoghurt and a banana all together.

We could sit anywhere, so Georgie and me found Archie and Jake and Dillon and we all took over our own table. Our activity groups were announced. Our group had all my friends in it. And Bonnie. We had to choose a bird name for our team, so we picked Cormorants, because they are dark and spooky.

After dinner we pushed all the tables against the walls.

Mr Goodman jogged and we all copied. "OK, so, in your teams, collect all the balls from this bucket and get them down to the baskets at the end. You can't use your hands, though. And if the ball touches the ground, you have to start again."

"That's impossible," Jake said.

"I'm not feeling very well," Archie said, so Miss Stewart let him sit out.

Mr Goodman lowered his voice. "So no running allowed for you, Maya." He glanced down at my leg. "Maybe you'd rather watch?"

Watch! I might as well get put to bed like a tiny baby! Mum must have told him not to let me do anything interesting, even though I had been allowed to join in PE lessons for weeks. And I'd done loads of swimming in the holidays.

"I'm going to do *everything*," I said. "I'm completely fine."

We had yellow balls. Jake tipped our bucket on its side so all the spongy balls rolled out. Georgie and Ellie helped pass the balls and ran around shrieking and bumping into people.

There were obstacles, cones and hoops to climb through. I used to love games like these.

I'm good with my arms. My arms are strong.

I got down on to the floor and used my elbows like chopsticks, with a ball clutched to my chest between my wrists. "Take it from me," I called.

Dillon bent down to collect my yellow ball, but his wrists slipped and the ball pinged off and rolled away.

"I'll be faster with Jake," he called and ran away.

I sat up. Dillon didn't want someone who couldn't run.

He wedged the ball under his chin and Jake's head squashed to one side to take it from him. Dillon and Jake kept going "Yesss" in a hiss and leaping and high-fiving each other and collecting one ball after another. They wouldn't pass the ball to me at all. Even when I stood in front of them they dodged me. Georgie had run off somewhere, so I couldn't pass to her either.

Rose's team were in the middle in a neat line, bending, passing balls and dashing to put them in the baskets. Maybe the balls they had were easier. I think ours were shinier so they slipped more.

Rose was going to be brilliant at everything.

I was rubbish. It was a waste of time I decided: people running around all over the place, teachers shouting instructions, people banging into each other. Bonnie just ran down the side of our team as if she was in a race all on her own.

Everyone looked like coloured sprinkles inside a snow globe when someone shakes it – when everything just goes crazy.

I sneaked outside with Archie in the chilly dark, so I could stroke Nibble. Nibble loved investigating the sleeve of my fleece. There were more stars in the sky in Wales. And these ones were more gleaming.

The only thing I was any good at was playing with hamsters.

Rose:
Trusting

The teachers had said we'd have time to read before we went to sleep but it was nearly nine o'clock and we were still in the cafeteria. I had been with people all day, and all the noise and being in a new place was making me feel jangled up.

Our team, the Eagles, won the game. Clemmy beckoned us all to do a lap of honour round the cafeteria, patting every table and leaping into the middle. "Eagles flying high!"

Mr Goodman laughed and said, "We just want you to get used to your groups. School Journey is all about teamwork."

"Does tonight's result count, though?" someone asked.

"We're all winners," Mr Goodman said. "It's just a bit of fun."

"Well," Clemmy said, "Miss Bruce definitely wrote down a score."

Clemmy did two celebration cartwheels, neat and fast. The whole place seemed to be full of spinning people now that the proper games had finished and some kids pulled each other down on to the floor and started wrestling.

Just as Clemmy went into a handstand, Miss Bruce stepped out and grabbed her legs. "There are far too many people here for you to be upending yourself, young lady." She shook her head. "Perhaps we all should move the tables back ready for breakfast tomorrow."

"Let's call her 'Miss Bossy Bruce'!" Clemmy whispered. "Anyway, there's bits of squished garlic bread on the floor. I actually mashed some in my hand! Yuck!"

Mr Goodman called, "Listening!" He did a handclap for everybody to copy. I copied it – *clap, clap, clap … gap … clap, clap.*

No one was listening. People were rushing and jumping and messing about. Poor Mr Goodman! His mouth twisted. His forehead creased and he looked around at all the wild children.

He clapped again.

I copied, and so did a few other children who were near, but most people weren't bothering. "Now, now … that's enough, guys," he called.

Some teachers have a special kind of energy inside them. Clemmy's mum, Julia, was like that. I wouldn't dare talk at the same time as Julia Pantock-Reid. You felt with her as if you mustn't breathe unless she said it was OK. Mr Goodman wasn't like that.

"Guys…"

He wasn't going to have any voice left.

I stood very still.

A sudden blast of a whistle sounded right beside me.

I put my hands over my ears. People made faces of agony.

Miss Bruce was the one blowing it. "That is enough!" she shouted.

Everyone went quiet.

"From now on, when you hear this whistle if you do not immediately stop what you are doing and stand completely still with your mouth CLOSED, points will be deducted from your whole team."

Mr Goodman rubbed his forehead. "Hilary, I don't think we need to be quite so…"

Miss Bruce ignored him. "I want to see every one of you sitting on this floor ready to continue in a count of five … four … three … two…"

We sat.

"Told you there were scores," Clemmy whispered.

Miss Stewart came forward. She had a necklace of chunky orange beads that swung when she moved. She opened her arms wide and looked at us with a smile, as if we were interesting friends.

The cafeteria was so quiet that you could hear the cross little whispers between Mr Goodman and Miss Bruce, just like Mum and Dad.

"I've got an idea," Miss Stewart said. "We'll do trust exercises. Find two more people and stand in threes, one person in the middle. Now face one person and have your back to the other."

Even though Miss Stewart had a soft voice, we all got up and did what she said.

"Close your eyes, middle people. Rock back on your heels, then forward on your toes. Your partners will be like a brake, stop you falling and push you gently back. Now try again, stepping a little further away."

Around the hall everyone was wobbling forwards and backwards with their eyes shut, like skittles, all hushed.

I stood opposite Clemmy, with Stevie behind, closed my eyes, and leaned forward.

"If you step too far away, the middle person won't feel safe and they won't relax," Miss Stewart said in a calm soft voice.

Back and forward – a soft push to tip me back, another soft push to send me forward again.

"Who do you trust?" asked Miss Stewart, her

voice like a spell. "You have to really trust someone to close your eyes and fall back or forward. It's a really important thing to be able to trust people, especially when you're in a team."

I peeped just for a second. Maya was on the other side of the cafeteria in the middle of a three. Her eyes were wide, staring back at me.

"I don't want *her*!" I remembered her shouting at Gran on that first day home from the hospital when we were going out for a walk, with Maya in her wheelchair. "She'll roll me off the kerb and break my teeth. Only you and Grandad. Get Rose away from me!"

Maya:
Not Going
to Sleep

At bedtime I didn't unpack, just pulled out what I needed. We were sardines: six of us squashed inside three lots of bunks. Bonnie had so much stuff with her. She'd brought loads of cuddly toys – no wonder her suitcase was so huge. I dive-bombed two teddies and a dragon off my top bunk and Bonnie threw them back.

Then Miss Stewart came in and said, "OK, lights out. See you all in the morning."

It was inky black. The shower dripped. A fly buzzed. It was really different to home, where you can hear all the traffic on the main road.

I reached in my rucksack for my torch, flicked it on and made police searchlights around the cabin.

I held it under my chin. "Whoooo are yooooou? Do I look evil?"

Bonnie giggled.

"Turn that off!" moaned Ellie.

We lay in the dark again.

"Let's tell ghost stories," I said.

"Let's not," Ellie said.

"You're boring," I said.

"You're annoying," she said.

"What do I do if I need the loo?" Bonnie

whispered.

Georgie sniggered. "You sneak out into the dark, by the sea."

"No, Georgie, don't tell her that. You use your torch and go to the bathroom through there, Bonnie," I said.

We all lay. I wasn't tired. I hadn't done a single thing all day apart from sitting.

"Where is Miss Bruce's cabin?" I whispered.

"She's in number four. That's only two cabins away. Do you think she's asleep?" Georgie asked.

"Yes, listen…" I did an impression of Miss Bruce snoring and everyone started giggling.

"Stop it! She might hear us," said Ellie.

I pictured Miss Bruce in her cabin unpacking. "Do you think she brought a teddy?"

Everyone laughed again.

"I'm really tired. I'm not talking any more," Ellie said.

"You just did," I said.

"Shut up!" everyone went.

Our cabin door whooshed open. Miss Stewart's head appeared. "Now, off to sleep all of you. No more chatting or you'll all be exhausted in the morning."

The door closed again.

"Miss Stewart is nice," I said.

Silence.

"Hey, do you think Miss Bruce keeps her boots on in bed?"

No reply. No one would talk to me even in a whisper. "You're all boring," I said.

Was Goody-Goody Rose asleep? She was bound to be. Rose always does what you tell her.

Rose:
The Cabin that
Smelled of
Christmas Trees

I had got everything ready for the morning before I got into bed. Clemmy had arranged with Miss Stewart that we would go to the Hang-Out and do laps and exercises before everyone else was up.

I think we were a quiet girl cabin, except for Clemmy. I could hear her in the bunk underneath me doing her relaxation exercises. "Tighten fists … and release. Pull in tummy … and release. Point toes, point, point, point." Then: "Are you doing them too, Rose?"

"Mmm," I murmured.

I wondered what our teachers were doing. Were they all in bed too?

I thought about Mum and Dad getting the message that we had all arrived safely, our bedrooms empty at home. And Gran getting on with her painting of the deer in the park. Would it be finished by the time I got home?

Maya didn't join in with the team game tonight.

Was she all right? My tongue made little stinging flashes round the bump inside my cheek.

Mum said I was a light sleeper. I didn't use to be. These days, when I was trying to get to sleep, my mind always began replaying Maya's accident like a film.

I was spinning again. My sister lay splayed like a star, her toes scudding over the sandy ground.

I hopped off and ran alongside the roundabout.

"Do it. Do it again!" Maya shouted.

My arms ached. My legs thundered as I pushed off, keeping wide of the sandy trench round the sides and leaping on.

Now Maya was warbling. She was always making stupid animal noises. I stared up into the spinning clouds, jumped down and whooshed us off again.

The cabin smelled like Christmas trees.

If only I could hear the sea.

Maya:
The New
Window Box

I sat up in bed in the morning and rubbed around the grey blob on the inside of my ankle where the biggest pin makes a bump.

Wake up, leg.

Stupid Leg is always colder than the other one. I got dressed and watched Rose and Clemmy jog off from the cabin next door for their special extra exercise. I pushed open their cabin door and sneaked inside. No one saw me in there, the others were too busy snoozing. Five seconds later, I was out again, holding one of Rose's new walking boots.

I woke Bonnie to help me.

A seagull came to watch.

"It's not food," I told the gull, scooping a little red plant out of the window box by our cabin door.

"Once there was a boot who wanted to be a plant pot..." I chanted.

The gull strutted around, keeping his beady eyes trained on us.

"Be quick!" I held the edges of the boot while Bonnie shovelled soil in around the thin green stem.

"The flower is still on," she said happily.

I stepped back to admire it. "Beautiful!"

We stared at the flower, all bright and nicely planted inside Rose's boot.

"Why are we doing this?" Bonnie asked.

"It's a good place for a flower."

"But…"

I held up my hand. "No more questions," I said gravely. "I like it."

Bonnie did a little skip. "So do I."

I added a tiny label, torn from my notebook and pushed between the leaves. "This is not a Rose bush!"

Try being perfect now, Rose!

I carried the new extra *window-box boot* to the cabin next door and shunted it behind the proper window box, where someone might see it, but only if they looked carefully.

Now to throw away the evidence. I ran back, kicked the sprinkled soil between the slats, and dusted off my hands.

"Come on, Bonnie," I called. "You're making us late for breakfast."

Rose:
Searching

I held out the one walking boot that I had found lying by the door.

"So you actually forgot to bring *one* boot?" Clemmy asked.

"I … I must have."

I'd searched right through the cabin and asked all the other girls, who were busy getting dressed. I even went to ask Terry the driver, and he said there was nothing left on the coach.

It didn't make sense. Unless…

Mum had taken me into town to choose them. They were in an extra carrier bag so if they got muddy they wouldn't make everything else dirty. I loved the red and black stripy laces. And they were exactly what the kit list said to bring.

Maya.

"I'll just have to wear my trainers," I told Clemmy.

"No. It's far too muddy. Honestly, Rose. It's a good thing you've got me. I've got some extra wellies Mum put in."

"But your feet are bigger than mine, aren't they?"

Clemmy tutted. "Well, thank *you*. I'm only trying to help!"

"Sorry, sorry, thank you. I will wear them," I said, checking under the bunks one last time.

Clemmy pulled a pair of huge lime-green wellies with sparkly stars from her case. "Maybe if I padded them a bit…" I said, looking for my extra pair of socks.

My head felt pounding and hot.

The day after my first competition, I hadn't been able to find my little trophy and then, later on, I found it in my bin, right at the bottom, after I'd searched everywhere.

Of course it was you, Maya. You refused to come to the shops with us. You said boots always rub your ankle.

I definitely wouldn't tell Clemmy, though.

Maya:
Bats and Bells

There was bacon and eggs and bagels for breakfast and you could help yourself to little pots of jam.

Archie yawned. He whispered to me, "Nibble wouldn't stop rustling in the night."

"That's what hamsters do, isn't it?" I said.

He nodded. "The other boys thought there was something alive, like bats, and kept putting the light on." He sighed. "This holiday is very tiring."

When breakfast was finished and he got up I realised he had his orange lunchbox under his coat.

"Archie. You can't take Nibble on the Sensory Trail."

"I can't leave him in the cabin, Maya," he moaned. "There's a cleaner ... with a big mop."

"But you can't wander around with a lunchbox."

One of the instructors jogged up to us. "You don't need to carry your lunch with you, mate. We all eat in the cafeteria."

Archie stared at me in frozen horror.

"My friend's got ... a special food allergy," I said. "He always carries extra supplies with him."

The instructor frowned. "Well, if you let the kitchen know, they could keep your special food in the fridge."

"Thanks," we both said.

"Right, get in your groups!" the instructor called.

Everyone was gathering.

Archie was panicking. "Nibble can't go in a fridge!"

We chose a tree behind a picnic bench and Archie wedged Nibble's box between two branches. We covered it with leaves and we were back with the groups before anyone noticed a single thing.

We found the Cormorants: Jake, Georgie, Dillon, Bonnie, Ellie, Hamza.

"We need a Cormorant greeting call," Dillon said. "How about, 'Peck, peck and something else'?" He pecked with his hands in a 'v' shape like a beak.

"Ark, ark?" Georgie suggested.

"Finding Cormorants in the dark," I added.

We practised, zooming at the other teams. "Peck, peck, ark, ark, finding cormorants in the dark!" I made up a stamping Cormorant dance.

"Cormorants are all black, aren't they?" Jake said. "How *do* you find a cormorant in the dark?"

"You don't!" Dillon laughed. "You wait for him to find *you!*"

Clemmy strode past us in a silvery white shiny jacket, white bobble hat and matching walking boots with pink fur-trim tops.

"It's a flamingo!" Dillon said. "Are you in the Flamingo group?"

"Shut up," she called. "You're just worried we're going to win again!"

"Quick. Cormorants to the front!" Dillon said, and we flew past Clemmy.

"There aren't any winners. Didn't you listen? We're actually in blindfolds, in fact," Clemmy called after us.

I pecked at Rose as I passed. She'd lined up with the Eagles group. She was stumbling in a pair of green wellies that were definitely the wrong size.

The instructors made us do jogging to warm up, and then we were each given a blindfold. "Put these on. This Sensory Trail helps you to experience the world in a new way," Mr Goodman said.

"Now, Bonnie, would you like to do the trail with the others and I'll stay nearby?" said Miss Stewart.

"Yes," Bonnie said. "You go away."

"I won't be far away, but I will try a blindfold," Miss Stewart said. "It's such an interesting thing to do."

A line of rope fixed to yellow posts led away into the trees.

I fiddled with my blindfold and tried it on top of my head as a hat. Bonnie made hers into a hat too. Then I pulled my blindfold on. The world went black. We twirled. I got dizzy straight away, spinning my arms out. "I'm a windmill. I'm a dodgem." I bumped into Dillon.

"Take hold of the rope in your left hand and put your other hand on the shoulder of the person in front," called out one of the instructors.

I felt for the rope with one hand and clamped my other on Dillon's shoulder.

"What if we tread on an unexploded bomb?" I said.

"There aren't any, Maya," Miss Stewart said.

"You don't know that. Maybe they just haven't exploded yet," I said.

People around me laughed.

I felt as if I might suddenly find a brick wall in front of me. I shuffled forward, feeling out with my toes for the next step, then the next. The ground felt squelchy, then bumpy. Dillon wriggled away from me. I waved my arm, checking.

"We could be anywhere," I told Bonnie. "We could be on the moon."

"It's best to stay one behind the other," said Miss Stewart.

"Any silly children will be sent back to the cabins," came Miss Bruce's annoying voice. "This is about listening, something some people are very bad at."

I pictured Miss Bruce upside down in a tree, falling out … slowly.

The rope began to go lower. I pulled down a tiny corner of my blindfold to peep out. A few people in front of me were crouching down. We were at an opening, like a big pipe. I got down on my hands and knees, let go of the rope and pulled the blindfold properly over my eyes again.

Hearing yourself breathe is a funny thing. I mean, you know you're doing it, but with a blindfold you really hear the breathing and you sound monsterish. The wet chill inside the pipe made me cold to my bones and it made Stupid Leg a bit jumpy.

"It smells of old monster fungus!" I called, banging against the chilly, hard sides of the pipe as I crawled along. "Don't breathe. We're all being poisoned!"

Lots of people laughed.

"Where are yooooooou?" I called to Dillon. My voice came out echoey and odd.

"I'm still in front of yooooooou!" he called back.

Some other voices went *woo* behind me and Miss Bruce snapped, "That is very silly!"

My trousers weren't waterproof. I pulled myself uphill, pretending to be a squirming creature. Wet chill was seeping in. My knees were soaked. I felt the ridge at the end of the pipe. The air changed to proper outside air.

I struggled to my feet. Now my knees had turned to squelchy babies' nappies. I found the rope. Off again!

A new sound began … bells chiming.

Stupid Leg started to ache. Something silky brushed my face. I reached out and touched the feathery hanging shapes. "Bats," I murmured. "Sleeping upside down. Can you feel their silky wings stroking your face?"

Bonnie gasped. "I don't like bats."

"It's OK. They're not real," I said.

The rope scratched along my palm as I sped along. The chiming got louder and louder until I was surrounded by it. Something long was put in my hands with a heavy end, a whacker. So I swung. All of me shuddered. *Bonggggg ... bonggggg...* It was so beautiful, playing bells. I whacked and whacked and whacked. Big deep bell, middle singing bell, high chiming Christmas bell... *Boooonnnnng ... bonggggg ...*

I was a bell now; all of me shook.

"Next person," a voice said, but I was still whacking and the banger was torn out of my hands.

"Aww ... that wasn't very long." I stood listening to the chiming and Bonnie's laughter. I waited for her. She wouldn't stop whacking either.

"You have to stop now and let someone else have a turn," a grown-up voice was saying.

I turned round, caught hold of Bonnie's coat and reached up to whisper. "Do you know how to be a wolf, Bonnie?"

Bonnie giggled. She was my pet.

I pulled off my blindfold. There were no teachers anywhere near us. I pulled off Bonnie's blindfold too and she blinked.

I put my finger to my lips. "Let's be wolves!"

Rose:
Meeting
a Wolf

Under my blindfold I was on my own. I could sort of drift away. Like a busy nocturnal animal: a mole or a fox, feeling my way, sniffing. I didn't peep once.

You are supposed to trust other people and I could tell from the voices and giggles that some people were being silly. Twigs snapped. I turned my head, listening out for swishes and rustles.

I loved playing the bells. They echoed so much! Wouldn't it be great to have a whole orchestra under the trees? I liked the hanging feathers too, like animal tails, and reaching up to feel them.

I heard Mr Goodman call, "Only another fifty metres, Hilary," which must have meant Miss Bruce. We were coming down a slope and Clemmy had just started to say, "After this we should have time to—"

And then there was a rushing noise beside me and a howl. "Aaaoooo!"

I stumbled. My chin hit Clemmy's back. My nose squashed against her furry hood. I scrabbled, grabbed and fell over on the muddy path. My blindfold came off. Everything was bright and the howling person was Bonnie leaping around us.

Miss Bruce called, "Oh my word," as Mr Goodman helped her up.

Behind a tree I noticed my sister, wide-open mouth laughing.

Maya! You always wreck things!

"Stop that noise! *What* are you doing, Bonnie?" Miss Bruce said furiously. She rubbed at a great big smear of mud on her coat.

Everyone else had finished the trail now and they were handing in blindfolds, watching us.

"I was being a wolf," Bonnie said, giggling. "And then you all fell over!"

Most of the class laughed.

Miss Bruce blew her whistle for silence.

Clemmy brushed her dirty coat with little angry strokes. "Maya made Bonnie do that, didn't she?" she asked me. "I am actually very angry and we could have been injured, Rose. She shouldn't be on this trip."

Maya was made to stand in front of Miss Bruce. She nodded and looked at her feet. She swung her bad leg too, as if it had got loose. That's what she always does when people tell her off.

Miss Bruce's voice got louder. "... responsibility!" I heard her finish.

My eyes met Maya's. She was staring at me with a look of hate. I felt a dizzy, wobbly jolt.

Had Maya been trying to stop Bonnie?

Maybe Bonnie had just jumped out, like it was a game that she'd made up herself.

"We don't *know* it was Maya's fault," I said.

"What?" Clemmy puffed and fumed. "Of course it was Maya's fault."

"It could have been Bonnie's idea." My words seemed to get quieter while Clemmy's face filled with fury. "I can't tell on her. I … I promised Mum I'd look out for her."

Clemmy stood with her hands on her hips. "You know it was Maya. You know lots of things you are not telling me, Rose Sheridan. It's pathetic. You don't have to bother looking out for your sister. She's on the lookout for you!"

Maya:
Being
Told Off

I studied my wellies. Miss Bruce was ranting at me. "Look me in the eye."

"It was a sort of game," I said. "I stayed with Bonnie so she didn't hurt herself."

I couldn't look in Miss Bruce's eyes, though. I decided they were actually poisonous and sent out chemical rays. Instead I stared at the place on top of her nose, right between her eyes.

"You are telling me you did not encourage Bonnie to run and be silly?"

I shrugged.

Mr Goodman appeared. "Bonnie is easily led…" he said. "You have to be more responsible, Maya." He ran his hand through his curly hair. "I won't have you spoiling the experience for other children."

I looked down at my feet again.

The mud on my boot looked like melted chocolate.

Why did Mr Goodman have to moan at me as well?

At lunchtime there was only cottage pie left when I got served. I hate cottage pie. It tastes evil and disgusting. I hid it under my knife and fork and Miss Bruce told me off again, marching up and down behind me, glaring. I still didn't eat it, though. She couldn't make me.

After lunch, we all set off to the island. It looked like a grassy hill with rocks around it, sitting in the sea. There weren't any trees. It had a little beach, like a skirt, and at the back there were caves, Mr Goodman said.

"Will you be OK with this, Maya?"

I scowled. "It's just a path."

Bonnie wasn't allowed to come with us, though. Miss Bruce was staying with her, so Miss Stewart could come with us instead.

"I want to be with Maya," Bonnie said.

"She'll see you later on – won't you, Maya?" Miss Stewart said.

Bonnie put on a massive sulky face.

"I could wave," I said. "I mean, it might not work but … if you watch, you might see me."

"That's a lovely idea. Bye now, sweetheart," Miss Stewart told Bonnie.

Rose:
The Gleam

When I went back to the cabin to get my rucksack I noticed an odd brown flowerpot outside our cabin with a red flower in it squashed up next to the window box. It was my boot. I lifted it up. It was dark and damp. And a scrap of paper was sticking out – but I couldn't read the writing.

I checked around me. I was alone, holding this mean trick.

You are pathetic and stupid and not funny, Maya!

If I could just smash something of yours… But you never look after your things anyway.

I took a deep breath. That's what Mum always said to do.

The stripy red and black lace was just dirty brown now. I had loved those laces and now that one would never look right. New things have a gleam. My boots had the gleam. Not now, though.

I scooped out the soil and cleaned the inside with paper towels.

Back with the group I told Miss Bruce I'd dropped my boot in a puddle. She said, "Silly girl." It looked old and bashed. It still felt wet inside.

We visited the coastguard's hut, where he was drinking tea. He talked to the teachers and we stared at the noticeboard, which explained about the tides and said things like "Safe to set off", with times.

I didn't tell Clemmy about my boot.

Maya:
Meeting Seals

Walking across the causeway meant clambering over scratchy rocks and it took nearly half an hour. Stupid Leg is always stiff for climbing. I used to be a good climber. Now I was as slow as a worm, watching Rose and Clemmy leaping ahead of me. We all spread out. None of my friends waited for me. I looked for the best route, trying not to trap my feet, sometimes grabbing on to a rock till I found the next place and even going back a bit when I got stuck and trying a new way.

All the time I could see the sea on either side and hear it whispering. Miss Stewart clambered over the rocks beside me. She said that all sorts of creatures survive in the rock pools because the tide comes up over the causeway and then they're under the sea again. "Seal Island is a place people have visited to do projects," she said, "and it's beautiful. We only have a limited time here." When Miss Stewart talked about islands and plants and things I could tell she really cared about them. She kept mentioning little facts. I looked back at the beach where we'd been yesterday and the sand looked very smooth, like a huge pale banana. The sheep on the slopes were like white insects. I wondered where Bonnie was now. I saw something purple on the grassy clifftop, so I waved at it. It might have been a purple sheep, for all I knew.

I liked the bright creatures in the rock pools. And finding a great big crusty anchor covered in mussel shells. When we reached the other side of the causeway I looked up at the grassy island.

Mr Goodman called, "Stand still, everyone," while he counted us. "We're going up on to the top, then round the back where the caves are for a talk from Miss Stewart."

We followed him up the path all the way to the top. The wind was buffeting me and I could see the whole of Whitesands on the cliff. I spun round with my arms open, collecting the wind. "This is the top of the world!" I shouted, because it was.

As we were coming down the back of the island someone saw a bird of prey and we all stopped to watch it hover. Miss Stewart said it might be an osprey. "If it is, those are rare. You're very lucky."

Miss Stewart told everyone to gather and started talking. I wasn't in a listening mood.

I sat a bit further away from the group, then a bit more. I was a rock-hopper. Soon I was on a big smooth rock on a bit of beach round the corner that was just mine. I looked out at the sea and scooped a handful of pebbles. I threw one, watching it arc down and *plop*.

Then, all at once, I felt completely certain that something was watching me. A head came up, smooth, shiny, speckled like a stone. Huge dark eyes. It bobbed about in the shallow water beside me. A seal.

I held on to the pebbles I had been going to throw and sat very still.

"Hello," I whispered.

The seal smiled. He really did. He had long dark whiskers and a shiny wet nose, a bit like a dog's, and the most amazing black marble eyes.

He had come to see if I was interesting.

"Are you on your own too?" I whispered.

I looked along the water's edge. Another flash of movement. A second seal was flopping on a rock on the beach a bit further along. It had flippers sticking out by its sides and a curled tail, and it was lounging exactly the way a mermaid would in a story. The seal in the water bobbed and swam around and pointed a flipper upwards, waving at me. I waved back. It flicked and disappeared under the water. The seal on the beach didn't look comfortable. It was lumpy, like a fat sausage. It jerked about and rolled and dragged itself around on the sand.

But then my first seal bobbed up again and when he swam he was so smooth in the water, making clever little turns and whooshes ... as if he was made of sea. It was his place. I felt like I was moving too, dancing in the water with the seal. I sat there on the island while seagulls made their sad cries over my head, and the seal and me seemed to be a hundred miles from the world in a secret pocket.

Voices began. The seal on the beach did a caterpillar flop and rolled into the water. My swimming seal's head dipped under and disappeared. For a moment I felt as if I had gone under the waves too. Why didn't all these noisy people just go away instead of invading *my* beach?

Jake wandered past me and threw a pebble in the water.

"Don't!" I said.

"Don't boss me, Maya," he said.

Miss Stewart wandered along the sand and sat on another rock, staring out to sea. "Did you see any seals, Maya? They get lots here. And at this time of year they come here to have their pups."

Pups! I looked for my seals again, but they'd gone. Or maybe they were watching from somewhere nearby.

"They're friendly creatures," Miss Stewart said. "Just keep your eyes peeled; it's easy to miss them. Some people say that creatures exist that are half man, half seal, called Selkies. There are many folk tales that tell of a Selkie who falls in love with a human, whose tail is locked away in a box and who yearns to return to the sea."

Everyone was noisy and chatting, wandering around me, filling my beach. Selkie. I liked that word. I whispered it to myself. No wonder the seals went somewhere quieter. But I wished I could see them doing their acrobatics in the water again.

"Do all the Selkies in the stories go back to live in the sea?" I asked.

"Some do. Some are trapped on land and sometimes their own kind are searching for them. In some stories they make a choice, or they can visit."

"I'm a silkie," Jake called.

"That's not the word," I said.

"If you were a sea creature, what sea creature would you be?" Dillon asked Jake.

"I'd be a wiggly octopus. Or a great white shark."

Georgie called, "I can see a seal."

We all looked at a mound of rocks where she was pointing.

"That isn't a seal, that's just a rock," Jake said.

"Come out, seals!" Georgie called. But the seals stayed away.

Clouds were rolling in over the island. Everyone else ran to the top and back while Mr Goodman counted. Rose and Clemmy did cartwheels on the sand. If I turned my head, I was on my own again, looking out at the rocky place where my smooth grey seals had been. "You can come out now," I whispered. But they didn't.

"We all need to head back while the causeway is still easy to cross," Mr Goodman told everyone.

"Quick!" people called. They all streamed away and back down towards the causeway.

I was last again.

"Come on, Mistress Maya. Wouldn't want you washed away," Mr Goodman called.

I wasn't frightened as I set off. The sea felt like an exciting friend. The waves were frothing at the edges of the path. Whitesands looked so far away, stranded on the cliff while the rolling sea grabbed the island back.

I turned back for a moment to whisper, "Goodbye."

Rose:
Running in
the Sea
and Sky

Mr Goodman jogged on the spot. We were down on the beach, back from the island. I suppose there was time spare before tea. "We're going to do a keep-fit challenge. Not in teams. You can do as much as you want. I'll demonstrate and the rest of you can copy. Stop when you've had enough."

We spread ourselves across the sand. There was so much space! We did press-ups and we all copied Mr Goodman, shouting out our totals and collapsing and laughing. Next we did star jumps. Clemmy said, "Rose and me can do the splits," but I don't think anyone heard.

It was so much more fun than normal PE, with all the leaping and jumping people. Then everyone started running between two big stones on the beach, and you had to pat each stone and keep score of the number of laps you did. The sand was very easy to run on. I leaped over beautiful long shadows. Gran loves to paint shadows, especially cloud shadows. She says the hardest thing to paint is the sea and sky, and she never gets tired of it. She puts in lots of colours you wouldn't expect. I ran along, feeling the sandy ridges, as if someone had combed the beach in a fancy design.

Clemmy came racing past and shouted, "You're

too slow, Rose!"

There were wide puddles further up the beach where the tide had come in. It looked as if the clouds had fallen down and collected in them, like the whole world spun upside down. The beach was turning to glass. I wished I could paint the shine, the purple bubbles, the sand flies puffing up around my feet.

I caught sight of Maya walking jerkily to sit in the dunes.

I stopped running.

I could go too. I could just sit with her.

Clemmy sprinted past me again. "You aren't making any effort!"

Maya was waving to someone. Archie. He used to be friends with both of us.

Are you making Archie laugh? You're so clever at making people laugh. Tickling. Chasing. It's that strange voice you put on. Once, when we were on holiday, you said the seaside place was a new planet and we made up strange crackly alien voices. That was so fun.

Clemmy came and jogged beside me.

I breathed a big gulp of air, gathered speed and pounded next to her down the beach.

Maya:
In Someone
Else's House

Mum would say, "*Just stop, you've done really well already.*" Her voice ranted in my head. "*You've had a really full day.*"

Stupid Leg plays tricks – lets me start then, all of a sudden, turns wobbly. Maybe my sister was sending mind messages – *OK, make her fall over … NOW!*

My arms are really strong from using crutches, so I was OK with the press-ups.

I stopped doing the challenge exactly when Rose and all the other laughing people started racing up and down between the two marker stones, down the whole length of the beach.

Georgie had been with Ellie nearly the whole day and she just said "hi" and ran past me. They were still grabbing each other and giggling and running.

I found Archie sitting in the dunes, but the minute I sat beside him he asked me to look after his lunchbox so he could go and run too. "I need to do the challenge, otherwise Mrs Olson keeps asking me what's wrong," he said. He could have talked to me a bit.

No one cared what I was doing. I took Nibble out and stroked him because no one was watching me anyway. Mrs Olson and Miss Stewart just sat chatting, and Bonnie was colouring something.

Nibble's soft fur made me remember being with Sammy, the dog from next door. I used to spend ages playing with him after school. But when I came back home from hospital after almost a whole month he leaped up and barked. He'd forgotten who I was.

There was something wrong about our house too; it had shrunk.

"You're as heavy as a sack of potatoes," Dad said as he carried me inside with my sticking-out green leg cast, past the shoes in the hall piled on the shoe rack.

I didn't need shoes.

The living room had felt very full of people. Dad lowered me on to the sofa and told Rose to find a cushion for my leg, and Mum rushed away to find some presents from people at school. Then Gran arrived, gathered me in her arms and burst into tears. "You're home!"

It still smelled of home ... Mum's grapefruit shampoo and cooking. But, when I stared around me, everything felt different: was our lounge always this colour blue? That coffee table, the stripy curtains, that lamp by the window.

This was someone else's house, I decided. Those weren't my family. They were just some people.

She wasn't my sister any more. Rose definitely was not my sister.

Now, when I looked to where the figures were all racing across the sand, I thought about Rose running: at sports day, in cross-country at school, everywhere. Rose runs in this neat way, like a deer in a park, her long legs flying.

I was always the runner. I was better at running than Rose. No one would believe it now, but it's true.

People made silhouette shapes – wide stars – leaping, freezing black against the sky. Rose and Clemmy started doing their stupid cartwheels.

Were the seals watching me? Had they swum over from the island? They didn't need to run.

Bonnie flopped down beside me. "I'm bored," she said.

I was pleased she'd come to find me. "We don't need *them*. I'll tell you a story," I said.

Bonnie's eyes opened wider. "Really?" She shunted up close.

A picture came straight into my head. "Once there was a seal who wanted to be a butterfly," I said.

"Why?" Bonnie asked, her face all serious.

"I can't tell the story if you interrupt. You have to listen," I said.

"I am listening."

"The seal wanted to be a butterfly because butterflies can fly. Anyway, there was a butterfly flying around her nose. 'Ooh, you are such a sausage blob. But I am so dainty and delicate and brilliant.' That's what the butterfly was like every day, showing off."

"So what happened?" Bonnie whispered.

"The seal watched the butterfly and she decided it couldn't be very difficult to fly, if you really wanted to. So, the next morning, she found the highest rock on the beach, because she had noticed that butterflies take off from high places and just spread their wings. So she flopped and flapped up on to the rock and waved her flippers, which weren't very big... *Ready, steady...* Her body filled with energy, she took a big breath, and then she threw herself off the rock. And just for the tiniest second she thought she was flying, but really she was falling, and she went bumping all down the rock and rolled on to the beach."

"Oh. What did the other seals say?" Bonnie asked.

"They just laughed at her. *Rawnk … rawnk…*"

Bonnie wriggled about beside me. "*Rawnk … rawnk…* Did she try and fly again?" She leaned heavily against me.

"I haven't got time to tell the next bit," I said.

"That's a really good story. I think she did try again. She did, didn't she?"

I liked that Bonnie enjoyed the story. "I'll tell you some more another day," I said. "I made that story up. Completely on my own."

I walked out towards the sea to the line where the shells got washed up. All the keep-fitting people were still running about. I began to search. Something funny? Smelly fish? That would be wet and disgusting. I hadn't seen very many, though. The eyes would be creepy. Some seaweed? Too boring. What about something alive? That could be exciting. Hard to catch, though.

When I found the right "thing", it was just about perfect. And it fitted so well in the plastic bag I'd brought, so it just looked as if I'd been collecting shells.

Run away, Rose!

Rose:
The Monster

After tea, we were allowed to be in the Hang-out with our friends. While Clemmy was in the loo, I picked out little bits of grit from inside my boot and cleaned it a bit more. If I polished it at home, it would look better, and the white streaks might come out. Grandad would know what to do.

We went to bed and I lay in the darkness, surrounded by all the loud-breathing girls. Gran says sea air makes people sleepy. Tasha definitely snored. I thought about the beach tonight with all the sparkling colours in the sea and sky.

I think I had been lying for about twenty minutes when I turned over and stretched my legs out to the cool end of the bed.

"Ow!" My leg shot back.

Something sharp had stabbed my big toe.

"Rose? You woke me up," Clemmy's sleepy voice complained from the bunk below.

Other voices joined in. "What's wrong?"

"Who shouted?"

I stayed curled up. "I think … there's a thing … in my bed." I wriggled my toe…

"Put the light on," Clemmy said. "Do it."

In the bright glare Stevie stood by the switch in blue pyjamas, her face caught in a screech like in films. "What is it, Rose?"

My heart pounded. I pulled off my whole duvet.

"Eugh!" We all flew to the edges of the room.

The crab had a pear-shaped thorny orange body and incredibly long legs like a spider. It was huge.

I clenched my fists. I bit down hard on the inside of my cheek. Tears sprang in my eyes. "I … I … I…"

"Oh, my God. Oh, my God. Is it alive?" Tasha whispered. "I'm getting Miss Bruce."

"How are you not running around screaming, Rose?" Stevie said. "There's a crab in your bed; it's not normal."

"Eugh, Rose, gross!" Clemmy said. She stepped back towards my bunk. "It's only got seven legs," she pronounced. "And it smells … like old shells in a bucket."

I stared at the patches of crimson and crusty mottled green on the crab's spiny back. It would take so many paint colours to try to blend that. "It's dead," I said.

Just a dead thing from another world. The crab didn't scare me now. I knew Maya had put it there.

"I'm getting a teacher," snapped Clemmy, heading for the door.

Maya:
The Viking Woman

I liked lying in bed waiting for a scream, all the excitement boiling. She might not scream, of course. I pictured her foot stretching. Rose sleeps curled on her side, but she would still find it.

I had to wait ages. I began to wonder if she was cuddling my monster creature instead. Maybe Rose had found a new best friend – ha! But then panicking voices started calling in the cabin next door, and then everyone in my cabin was waking up, asking, "What is it?"

Georgie ran off to investigate. Then she was back. "Something horrid happened in Cabin Three," she called. "Quick, everybody!"

We all rushed out into the moonlight to find Clemmy and Rose and everyone racing out of their cabin. Then more people popped out of lots of other cabins. Some were in bedclothes, some had duvets wrapped round them. Mr Goodman arrived in stripy blue pyjamas and his sweatshirt, Miss Stewart in a huge fluffy yellow dressing gown.

Then I saw Miss Bruce with wild tall hair striding out from Rose's cabin with "*the thing*" dangling from her hand gripped in a sock.

There was a lot of laughing and screams.

"Eugh!" "I can't look!" "What is it?"

"Be quiet!" the teachers shouted.

Miss Bruce had to blow her whistle because we were all enjoying it so much. And then they did a quick register in case some of us had disappeared as well. Then Mrs Olson fussed over Rose's toe in case it had dropped off.

My prehistoric crab looked as big as a teapot, its claws hanging down. Long pincers. Crusty shell. Hanging off Miss Bruce's hand as if she was a snack.

Rose stood beside Clemmy, looking right at me.

I stared back. *Did your beautiful toe feel a sharp nip?*

Miss Bruce had a big rug over her shoulders and I whispered to Bonnie, "Miss Bruce has turned into a Viking."

"Who knows about this?" she shouted. "I want an answer. Who knows about this?"

"It's a crab, Miss," one of the boys said.

"I am fully aware it's a crab. How did it get into Rose's bed?"

"Maybe it was looking for the sea," someone suggested.

"Maybe it crawled in," Ellie said.

"It's dead," Stevie said.

"Maybe it crawled in and then died," Ellie said.

"It was in the top bunk, you idiot!"

"Now, now," called Mr Goodman.

"It stinks. It's been dead for ages," Stevie said.

"Rose could have been badly injured," Clemmy said. "Rose knows who did this. You do, don't you, Rose? Tell them!"

I made my face look mild ... surprised ... interested. I studied the window box beside me as if it was the most interesting window box anyone ever saw.

Rose's eyes had been on me but now she was staring at the ground. She shrugged. "No idea," she said.

No one could stop staring at my magnificent dangling crab. I wished it was alive and biting.

"Maya?" Miss Bruce stared at me hard. "I suspect *you* know something."

I gave her a look, eyes wide. "That's not fair, Miss. Why do you just assume it's me, Miss?"

I looked again at Rose. *Dare you to tell. You won't, though!*

We all waited. To pass the time people hung off

the bannisters and pulled hoods over their heads and Felix began chasing Hamza round a cabin until Mr Goodman told them off. He yawned and rolled his eyes towards Miss Bruce.

She sighed. "We're not going to get to the bottom of this tonight," she said. "But I do suspect foul play."

"Ooh, Sherlock!" someone murmured.

Miss Bruce stared hard in the direction of the comment, but I don't think she was sure who had said it. She pulled her blanket round her shoulders and swept all of us with a look of ice. "I do not take kindly to being woken by *silly* children playing tricks. Now, get to bed, all of you."

Rose:
Confusing

Our cabin was full of chatting.

"Wasn't Miss Bruce's hair funny?" Stevie said.

She and Pip started giggling.

Clemmy steered me to our bunks. "You have to tell me," she whispered. "All of it." We climbed up, sat under my blanket. I found myself shaking. I kept picturing the way Maya had just looked at me, that glare. Like I was her enemy.

"M-M-Maya threw an egg at me, the day we left," I said.

Clemmy clutched my arm. "This is worse than I thought. What kind of egg?"

"A boiled egg." I spoke the words quietly, right by her ear.

"I see. Did she throw anything else? The plate?"

"No … you don't understand."

Clemmy leaned against me. Her hair tickled my nose. "Did you throw one at her?"

"No."

"Did anyone see?"

"No. My gran. But Maya said her hand slipped."

Clemmy nodded. "Mmmm. Your gran probably suspects."

People began getting into beds.

"There's things she does, when we're at home." I

breathed out with the relief of telling. "She messes up my room. She tips things on the floor and moves things and changes the books round so they aren't in alphabetical order."

"You need to lock the door. Or get a webcam. What else?"

"She was the one who took my boot."

"I knew it. I knew you wouldn't have left it at home. Well, you'll never see it again. She should pay for it."

"No, I found it. She put a geranium in it."

"A geranium?"

"It's a flower."

"I know what a geranium is."

"She put it with the window boxes."

There was a moment of breathing. Clemmy was deciding something.

A wave of sadness seemed to swallow me. I gulped. "I don't know what to do. It started when … I … when she hurt her leg… She's always thought…"

"When are you two ever going to bed?" Stevie moaned from the other side of the room. I realised the others had gone quiet. Maybe they were even listening.

The light went out.

Clemmy's grip tightened. "Your sister is a monster, Rose," she hissed. "She should be in a different school for bad children. Now you've told me we'll talk to Mr Goodman and he'll tell the other teachers."

I pulled away, horrified. "No. No. We can't tell anyone."

"What?" Clemmy's voice was suddenly louder. "We have to."

"Go to bed!" Stevie moaned.

"In a minute," Clemmy snapped. And then to me, hushed: "We have no option, Rose."

I pushed her away. "I just wanted to tell you, but now I have we're not doing anything else. Just go to bed."

"Well, I'm telling." Clemmy pulled away. "And you can't stop me."

She set off down the ladder.

Panic filled me. I craned down. "If you tell, I'll say you made it up."

The bed creaked as Clemmy lay down.

"At last!" Stevie called.

Silence.

What would Clemmy do? I shouldn't have told

her anything.

I tried to breathe out … ten … nine … eight … but the panic rose and flowed around inside me.

Out of the dark Clemmy's voice whispered furiously from the bunk below. "You're weird, Rose Sheridan. That crab could have eaten your whole leg off and you still wouldn't tell on your precious sister!"

Maya:
Puff!

We were all snoozing now.

That was FUN! I pictured Rose's face. Definitely fun. And Miss Bruce. And my crab could be in a crab museum.

I snuggled in my warm bunk and listened to the shower. *Drip ... drip ... drip ...* I thought about the way seals swam, curling in the water.

I wriggled a bit. I listened to everyone breathing. *Tap tap.*

A voice outside. "Maya...!"

I sprang awake, climbed down and tiptoed to the door. "Who is it?"

"It's me, Archie," came a whisper.

I scrabbled and opened the door. "Wassup?"

Archie's hair was all fluffed up. He stood there in his pyjamas and school fleece holding out his lunchbox as if I was a lunchbox inspector. "It's Nibble. He's being so noisy. The other boys can hear him rustling. They said it must be the Beast of Whitesands, and they keep putting the lights on."

"So what can *I* do?"

"Could you have him, just for tonight? I could have him back tomorrow."

I stared at Archie's pleading face. "Can't you

just show him to them?"

"Oli Palmer would tell the teachers. He hates my guts – he'd love to get me in trouble."

I think Archie was nearly going to cry.

"What's the matter?" Georgie's head poked round the door beside me.

We explained in hushed voices about Nibble being too noisy.

"We'll have him – of course we will. And we can explain to the others. They'll all help," Georgie said.

"What about Bonnie, though?" Archie whispered.

I peeped back inside and checked her curled-up shape. "It's OK. She's asleep already."

I took the box. "Go on then. Just for tonight, though."

When Archie had gone we whispered to the others about Nibble coming for a holiday and then everyone went to bed. I stroked Nibble for a while. Hamster noses twitch so much. And I loved the tickly feeling when he ran up my arm. I put the lunchbox in the bathroom. "We won't hear him in there."

"This is fun. I wonder what else is going to

happen tonight," Georgie said.

We grinned at each other and went to bed.

✗

"Eeek!!" A high-pitched scream.

The cabin went bright as the lights came on.

"What ... who?" I tried to wake up.

"Eeek!"

Georgie was by the light switch. I blinked. The other girls in the cabin were sitting up in bed.

"Maya!" Bonnie was in the bathroom doorway screaming. "There was a thing. I saw it. With my torch. In the box. Argh!!!!"

I flopped down out of my bunk. "It's OK, Bonnie. Shush, it's just a—"

The door crashed open. "What now?" Miss Bruce loomed in the doorway in her terrible night-time outfit, her hair even wilder this time.

"Am I to have *no* sleep?" she bellowed.

"A furry little thing. It was in a box," bleated Bonnie. "Then it ran..." Her chest rose and fell with gulps.

"What box?"

Everyone looked sort of frozen, like people in a play.

I didn't want Miss Bruce to find out about the

lunchbox. Archie would be in big trouble.

"Bonnie means she saw a mouse. I was feeding it… I found it by the sea and brought it back," I said quickly.

"You … you *what*?" Miss Bruce demanded. "Where is it now?"

"It ran away," Bonnie said sadly.

Miss Bruce turned her furious eyes on me. "Thank goodness those girls in the cabin next door came to find me. I will *not* have you messing around in the night, Maya Sheridan." She was exploding and puffing. "Well, you will suffer the consequences."

Everyone was staring. What was she going to do to me?

"Pack your things. You will spend the rest of your holiday sharing a cabin with *me*, because I do not put up with *silly* girls on School Journey. We'll see how much longer this behaviour lasts when you don't have an audience. You have one minute to gather your things. And the rest of you, straight back to sleep. I don't want to hear another peep out of anyone!"

The door slammed shut.

"Oh, Maya!" Georgie wailed.

"Find Nibble," I hissed. "Put him back in his box. We'll give him back to Archie in the morning."

"I'm waiting," came Miss Bruce's voice from outside the door.

So I had to walk to Miss Bruce's cabin with all my clothes and my towel and my duvet in a big pile, like an execution – my last walk as a free person. As I passed the cabin next door I saw two faces staring out of the window: Rose and Clemmy. Then I knew: it was *them* who had gone to get Miss Bruce. If I could have made jet rockets with my eyes, I would have frazzled them as I went past. Traitors!

Miss Bruce's cabin door closed.

A wall of heat hit me and a horrid sweet lemon smell. A washing line of clothes was hanging up between the door and the window. A huge bra whacked me in the face as I crossed to the only set of bunk beds.

"Straight to bed," Miss Bruce growled.

She turned away and ran water into the sink. "You will not disturb me again."

"No, Miss." I was very quiet and small now.

"Get in the top bunk."

I climbed up the steps and lay down.

Miss Bruce got in below me and the whole bunk lurched.

Grunt.

I was trapped.

The bunk rocked. I closed my eyes. Miss Bruce breathed in big puffs, like a person blowing out candles on a cake. My arms and legs felt hot and heavy and achy. The lemon smell was like the spray they use in school when someone has been sick in the corridor and it was taking away all the air. Stupid Leg started tingling. I couldn't get up. I couldn't move around, could I? I pointed my toes up and stretched my leg out, rubbing the skin around the metal bolts, little tingly sparks going off.

"Puff," from Miss Bruce.

My sister ruining my life. Again.

Rose:
"She's That
Kind of Person"

Maya had seen us watching when she went past with Miss Bruce. She was carrying all of her bedding. How terrible. I should never have looked out. Now she would think it was me who had got Miss Bruce, when it had been Clemmy.

Clemmy's voice was stern and pleased. "Maya gets herself in trouble, Rose. She's that kind of person."

"You've made everything worse," I said.

"Are you two *ever* going to bed?" called Stevie.

"We are now," Clemmy said, ignoring me and skipping back to lie down. "It's good if she shares with a teacher, Rose. It serves her right."

I climbed slowly back into bed.

There was nothing I could do, was there?

I lay down and pulled the duvet and blanket up over my head. Imagine being in a cabin all on your own with just a teacher. Would you have to clean your teeth at the same time as her? You wouldn't be able to get away.

Maya must be so furious. She would hate me even more.

Maya:
Total
Disaster

Next morning, when the breakfast bell rang, Miss Bruce said I could find some clean socks and I rushed straight back to my cabin to sort out the Nibble crisis.

The air froze as I walked in. Georgie and the others all sat round an empty lunchbox with glum faces. Georgie said, "Oh, Maya, after Miss Bruce took you away we all searched and it was useless. We never found Nibble. We just ended up going back to sleep."

I stared at the empty lunchbox beside her on the bed, with its bits of old salad and hamster bedding. Total disaster!

The door flew open and there was Archie.

"Archie, we're really sorry," Georgie said. "Nibble ran away and we never found him."

Archie's face crumbled. "But you said you'd look after him, Maya!"

"I did... We all did," I said.

"So where is he?" Archie asked coldly.

"I told the others to find him," I said. "Miss Bruce made me stay with her. I've only just come back. I thought ... I thought... Why didn't you find him, Georgie? He must have been in the bathroom."

Georgie shook her head. "Don't blame us. He isn't anywhere. We looked really hard, didn't we?"

Everyone nodded.

Archie was trembling. "You promised, Maya."

"We'll find him *now*," I said. "He can't have gone out, can he? Keep the door shut. He's in here somewhere."

We searched everywhere. We put all the suitcases on the beds and emptied everything out of each one.

Bonnie watched us, teary-eyed. "I didn't know. No one said."

"Be quiet, Bonnie," Georgie snapped. "There's no point crying now."

"It's not her fault." I hugged Bonnie. I couldn't bear thinking of Nibble and his soft warm little body. "He might just be curled up asleep somewhere, Archie," I said.

Archie shook his head. "It's like when he disappeared at home. We'll never find him now. He could be miles away." He poked at Nibble's bedding. "I will never forgive you," he said, looking at me.

I gulped. My chest filled with sadness. But I'd tried to help. It wasn't my fault. "Fine. Don't then," I said. "You shouldn't have brought him if you couldn't take care of him."

Everyone went quiet.

"You shouldn't speak to Archie like that," Ellie said.

"What about the way he spoke to me?" I said.

"He's really upset," Georgie said.

"So am I. I had to share with Miss Bruce," I said. "Nobody even cares about *that*." Words tumbled out of me. "Next time, look after your own hamster."

Everyone seemed to breathe in suddenly. "Maya!"

"Next time I'll find a better friend," Archie said.

And he walked out.

"If you had looked properly last night, none of this would have happened," I told Georgie.

"I beg your pardon? Right. I'm not staying in here with you," Georgie said, diving off her bed and rushing for the door.

It was all a mess. And I couldn't spend any more time looking because Miss Stewart knocked on the door again and told us to hurry up for breakfast.

Poor Nibble. What would he eat? Someone

might tread on him.

I kept gazing at things in the cafeteria – an unusually shaped hair scrunchy, the curl of a buckle, hats on chairs – willing them to be Nibble. Everything looks like a hamster when you've lost one.

Rose:
An Accident

"Just stop. She's not your sister." I put my hands over my ears. "Don't say any more."

I walked ahead of Clemmy over to the cafeteria.

Maybe I could still tell Maya it wasn't me. I could explain.

Maya was on her own in there near the door. She looked up. Her eyes were so angry and red; they made me freeze.

"I … I…" I couldn't say anything. "Maya, I…"

No. It was useless.

"Rose!" Clemmy said, yanking my arm.

We sat by the windows on the opposite side of the room. I gulped down three mouthfuls of cereal, then just fiddled with the spoon.

Maya was never on her own.

Maya had been crying.

I watched. She had a plate in front of her, but she wasn't eating. She kept staring at the floor. She had moved the chair back and seemed to be searching for something under the table.

I looked out of the windows at the early-morning sun on the beach.

Clemmy jabbed my arm. "If you don't eat your cereal you won't have energy for the day, Rose."

I pictured picking up my bowl and tipping the

entire contents over Clemmy's head.

What was I thinking? I was turning into Maya!

✗

Today's morning activity was making a shelter that three people could sit inside. My Eagles team didn't agree on how we should do it. Well, really it was Clemmy not agreeing with everyone else.

"The others are taking all the stuff!" Clemmy said furiously, pointing at everyone raiding the pile in the middle of the beach.

"We don't need a lot of stuff. If we all dig, we can make a big hollow," Joe said. "And just use some driftwood for the insides."

"Digging?" Clemmy put her hands on her hips. "That's just … ridiculous."

"We made shelters in Scouts," Joe said. "It's the best way."

"Really?" Clemmy did a long sigh.

"Well, I think it sounds a good idea," Tasha said.

Clemmy tutted. "Digging is a bad idea actually. I'm team leader and I say we build the shelter over there, where it's flat." She pointed to a patch of sand near the sea.

"You aren't the leader," Marcus said. "Who said you were?"

"OK then, loser, let's vote," Clemmy said.

We voted. Clemmy got two votes, me and her, and Joe got six votes from everyone else.

I gazed along the big wide bay with tiny people at the other end of it, and the blue sea and little waves coming in, because it was better than looking at Clemmy.

"That's it then; we dig. I just want to make a good shelter," Joe said.

We all looked for things to scoop with. I found a curved bit of wood.

"Well, I don't care any more." Clemmy leaned into a stretch with her arm over her head.

"Stop being a windmill and help," Joe said.

"I have to warm up," Clemmy said.

The rest of us dug. Sam and Barney did collecting.

We scooped out a hole in the side of the sand dune.

"Why don't you do some actual digging instead of just saying it's not going to work?" Tasha said to Clemmy.

"Because it's such a bad idea," Clemmy said. She wandered away.

Mr Goodman came jogging up. "Looking good," he said, and jogged off again.

I liked scooping. After about ten minutes, the sides fell in and Marcus, Joe and I got buried. We started again.

"Could we dig to the centre of the Earth?" Willow asked.

"Don't be an idiot," Joe said.

But I liked that idea.

I felt as if I was making a nest for giant birds. The sand was quite cool and wet deeper down and it fell in ragged curtains. We packed it into heaps and pushed it into a big pile to one side.

We stood up in the bright light. Half an hour of digging made a big pile. Phew. My back ached. I shook my head and sand flew everywhere.

We began to make the sides strong, wedging bits of wood inside to hold the roof up. I squirmed into the hollow and passed lengths of wood to Joe and Marcus. We kept swapping round. It was fun, even when sand leaked down on to me.

Our shelter was squashed into the side of the dune, ready for some very small people.

Clemmy appeared again. "Mr Goodman said two more minutes. Our shelter is actually not that bad," she said. "I've decided to be the first visitor."

She crouched down, crawled inside our shelter

and sat looking out.

"Are you having a picnic in there?" Joe said. I think he was quite pleased Clemmy liked it, though. "How about we each take turns sitting inside?" he said.

"There might not be room," Clemmy said.

"So you get out then," Marcus said. "*We* made it."

"In a minute," Clemmy said.

The teachers were waving to us from the middle of the beach. People were stepping back to admire their shelters, which were like strange broken garden sheds after a storm.

An excited brown and white dog caught my eye as it bounded towards us. It made happy dancing shapes, leaping in the air to catch a stick. Then I realised the person throwing the stick was Maya. She started running in loops, weaving nearer us.

Animals always love Maya. She's always nagging Mum for a dog.

The stick flew inside our shelter beside Clemmy. The dog bounded after it.

Mr Goodman blew a shrill blast on the whistle, yelling, "Everyone stop now!"

Clemmy kicked out. "Get it out!"

The dog barked and leaped around.

The side folded. *CRUMP*. Sand buffeted out and our walls collapsed. Clemmy and the dog both leaped out covered in sand.

"Whoops!" Maya called.

The dog ran away into the sunshine and danced a circle.

We all stared at our ruined shelter. It just looked like a junk pile beside the dune now.

"Bad dog!" Maya called in a jokey voice.

"You complete and total cow!" Clemmy shouted.

Everyone began shouting now. Teachers were coming over.

Maya's eyes found mine. "It was an accident."

I felt a hit of pain, like a thump deep inside me. An accident. If only I could grind that word up into little pieces and throw it far away somewhere.

I was back … that tight warbling noise … the spinning clouds … my arms jarring *thud* as I struck the metal bars in the middle … Maya's squeal.

The roundabout juddering. Falling off.

My sister lying like a strange puppet, her leg stuck underneath. Dad running up. Maya like a floppy screeching baby.

I was back in the hushed family room in hospital

… and hearing Dad's whisper to Mum, "Rose gave that roundabout an *extra push*. Why would she do that?"

The sky was a beautiful clear blue and the sea was folding, lapping in and out.

"Do something, Rose! It was her fault!" Clemmy said.

"No," I said. "No, it was my fault."

Maya:
Maya Made
From Stones

We'd had burgers and pasta for lunch and some cherry cheesecake, which was actually delicious. I peered at the cafeteria floor, still hunting for Nibble between the swinging legs. He must be so hungry.

"Now, listen up," called Mr Goodman, "for this afternoon's activity I'm going to give you a list of things to find. Miss Bruce and I will be on the beach standing by the markers. It's all about teamwork, guys. Have fun!"

He said we had to find these things: a perfectly round stone, five types of shell, a piece of driftwood, a piece of charcoal, a sea thistle, seaweed and an unexpected object.

We spread out. There was so much beach and wide sky. It felt warm in the sun.

Georgie still wasn't speaking to me. And Archie wasn't speaking to anyone. We wandered along the beach for a while. Jake grabbed his leg and moaned that something had bitten him, but he's always making up stuff like that. I couldn't even see where my sister and her group had gone. Maybe they'd been swallowed by a whale.

The five shells were easy. Dillon held on to our collection. We kept finding more that were better and chucking our others away, except for Bonnie, who was picking them up and stashing them in her handbag. Miss Stewart came up and said, "You're going to be with me now."

"I want to be with Maya! Can't I just stay for a while?"

"You'll see her later," Miss Stewart said, steering Bonnie away.

"I'll get you some more shells," I told her.

I was a bad influence.

After I watched them go, I found a long stick and combed a face in the sand and made hair with some seaweed.

I wrote 'MAYA' and filled the letters with little stones, so you would see it from high up. As I searched for stones for my 'MAYA' I found a long bit of charcoal, which is really just old burnt wood. I rushed over to Dillon who was grabbing handfuls of stones by the water's edge.

"Charcoal," I said. "I just found it."

He turned it over in his hands. "I thought all you did was muck about and lose us points."

I swallowed a big gulp of hurt. "No, I don't."

"Look, Miss Bruce said, after the Sensory Trail, that all the groups were neck and neck. But they must have taken marks off you and Bonnie for messing about. And then this morning…"

I nodded. "Sorry, Dillon."

His brow furrowed. "I've been wondering if maybe we don't lose marks for Bonnie. Maybe we even get extra marks for having her in our team."

I drew a curve in the sand with the charcoal. "Bonnie's … all right."

Dillon clenched his fists. "You have to take this more seriously. I heard there's prizes at the end of the holiday for the group who win."

"Prizes?"

Dillon's face was bright and excited. "Yeah. Someone even said there are Whitesands hoodies."

"I didn't know that," I murmured.

We both looked over the sea to the island. The sun was lighting the top bits gold, so it looked like hair on someone's head.

"So what do we still have to find?" Dillon asked. "Driftwood's easy. The whole beach is covered in it."

"Thistles. They're on the dunes," I said. "I'll go."

I walked away from the sea up towards the

hummocky dunes. I'd made Dillon fed up. I'd messed around and not been good in our Cormorants team. Stupid Leg dragged, heavy and achy. I was like a very old horse ploughing a wet boggy field ... *plod plod*.

"Maya!" Bonnie was calling me.

Miss Stewart was sitting with her, pointing out things in her book, *The Sea Shore*.

"I just need a thistle," I said.

Miss Stewart held up her book. "Let's check," she said.

She pointed to a picture of a thistle and started to read "Thistles are found..." I just wanted a thistle; I didn't want a whole lesson.

Dillon's head appeared over the long grass as he came racing up the slope in big bounds. "Everyone's finished finding their objects, Maya!" he called. "You're too slow!"

Rose:
Sea Thistle

Clemmy was still furious and stamping about Maya. We marched across the beach collecting the objects and I couldn't even hear the sea any more.

She just wouldn't stop. "Some babies throw their dinner. Your sister is like a wicked baby who never grew up, Rose. She hates you. And she's getting worse. One day they will write about her when she does a massive crime and you'll have to admit she's your sister."

"Please, Clemmy…"

"What will she do next, Rose? She might do anything. She's on the loose!"

"Stop saying bad things." I pressed the sides of my head where the pain was pulsing.

"You might discover she's not really your sister at all… Maybe she's adopted. Or maybe *you're* adopted."

"Clemmy!"

"That's it. She found out she's adopted!"

"Stop it!" I stumbled away from her across the sand.

"We have to tell the teachers all the other bad things she's done before it's too late."

"No, we don't. I don't want to talk about her any more."

I speeded up over the dunes. I had to get away from Clemmy's whining.

I stumbled into Miss Stewart with Bonnie. "Sorry," I mumbled. She held something out to me. "Look," she said, smiling. "This is a sea thistle." She pointed to them growing among the grasses. "You could sketch one, Rose."

Clemmy came bustling up behind me.

I'd never looked at a thistle close up before. It was so spiny and intricate, like a cactus. It really stung my fingers. I loved the colour – like grey-blue mist.

Clemmy's face set firm. "We have to get back with our objects, Rose." Her voice filled my head.

I sat down. "In a minute. I want to sketch." I thought of Gran. "You should sketch in the place you see something, because some of the feelings are different. Gran says you capture a special mood." I opened my little watercolour pencil set and the sketchbook Gran gave me. I breathed slowly. I looked out towards the sea and felt the waves moving forward and back like breathing... Out ... in ... out.

Clemmy's mouth puckered into her cross pout. "If there's extra time, we should be exercising. We said we would exercise every day to be the best we can be."

I poured some water into the little dipping pot and set it in the sand beside me. "I dug the shelter this morning," I said.

"That wasn't really a full-body workout, Rose. My mum…"

"Just go. I'm going to sketch thistles," I said.

I kept my eyes down and dipped my brush.

"We need to be ready for the Talent Show. I'm disappointed," Clemmy said, blotting out the sun.

That's what grown-ups always say.

I half closed my eyes, holding my thistle tight. I loved the way the grey and blue spines seemed to change colour to greens and purples when I turned it.

In, out, in, out, went the sea far below me. I took out a pencil and drew a soft line on my white page.

The grass swished as Clemmy walked away.

Maya:
Never Do This
With Charcoal!

Walking back up the path up to the doors of the education centre, my Cormorants team turned into a cross arguing swarm.

Dillon moaned at me. "It's your fault, Maya. You just drew names and faces on the sand!"

"I didn't know we had to be quick," I said.

Dillon rolled his eyes. "You don't listen."

"Why are you only blaming me?" I said. "I did try. I got the thistle … and the charcoal."

So unfair!

"She did get the charcoal," Jake chipped in. "And our shells are good. Maybe they give more points if your objects are better."

"What's so special about charcoal?" Georgie snapped. "Mr Goodman already said my starfish was a perfect specimen."

We pushed open the doors to find all the groups gathered inside, with teachers ticking off their registers.

Mr Goodman did a complicated hand clap for everyone to copy. "Now. Welcome, everyone, and thank you for adding to our spectacular display of the life of Whitesands beach."

The Cormorants all scowled and added our objects to the long table display.

The table smelled of pongy sea and the team names were written in front of each collection. I called out, "Hey, Jake, didn't you wash your socks?" and got some laughs.

The Skylarks had found a beautiful blue glass bottle. There were lots of good shells. Ours was the only starfish.

I could see the Eagles' bit of charcoal and it was nowhere near as good as my bit. It was right by my hand near the edge of the white cloth. Suddenly I had an idea. The teachers were all talking to each other by the doors. What if no one had come round to decide the winners yet?

I slid my hand up and felt the rough black chunk between my fingers. I rolled it slowly to the edge of the table and … into my pocket.

"Can I go to the loo?" I asked Miss Stewart.

"Of course," she said.

In the bathroom I dropped the charcoal into the toilet and flushed it.

The charcoal bobbed around. It was still there on top of the water. Hmm. I waited till the toilet had filled and flushed again. I added some toilet paper. Third flush. The water came up high.

Oh no, oh no.

It did a big kind of toilet gulp and the charcoal and toilet paper disappeared, and the toilet went on making a busy swallowing noise. I tiptoed out back to the room where Miss Stewart was explaining about types of sea creatures and how they move and feed.

I looked for Dillon and wandered around until I was beside him, staring at the loaded-up table. It looked a bit like a big dinner, but with nothing to eat. "The Eagles didn't collect any charcoal," I whispered.

"What?"

"Look." We stared at their area on the table. "They missed one item." I grinned at him. "And my charcoal's the biggest one and Georgie found a brilliant starfish."

"Are you sure their charcoal didn't fall on the floor?" Dillon muttered.

Miss Bruce turned to glare at us. "You two children are supposed to be listening. This is a really interesting talk."

Miss Stewart held up a razor shell and began saying something about them.

I hopped around from foot to foot.

At the end of the talk Dillon went straight to the

teachers with me marching behind him.

"No one said who the winners were and we were wondering who the winners are?"

Mr Goodman smiled. "Well now, Dillon. It's not always about winners and losers."

"I know, it's just that we tried really hard and ... I've just noticed that the Eagles team didn't find all their objects."

Beside Mr Goodman Miss Bruce frowned. "What do you mean, Dillon?"

Dillon pointed at the table. "The Eagles team didn't collect any charcoal. Do they get disqualified?"

Miss Bruce's face turned red. I felt a bubble of worry start in my stomach. "Come over here, young man," she said. "Show me."

"See?" Dillon pointed at the table.

"Yes, I do see." Miss Bruce's face changed to a snarl. "The Eagles team brought all their objects to me to check while we were still on the beach, so I know they found a piece of charcoal. Someone has decided to remove it from this table."

She sounded so angry that everyone stopped talking.

"I ... I ... it wasn't me." Dillon's mouth froze. He

pointed at me. "It was Maya. She told me."

Mrs Olson came rushing up. "Something's wrong in the girls' toilets. Water's flowing out of the door."

I wished I could disappear in an explosion, like a firework. *Puff* … gone. Everyone was staring at me. Everyone guessed I'd lied. Dillon didn't even try to help or say it was a mistake. He just told them it was me.

"I'll deal with this." Miss Bruce marched me away to sit on a bench by the doors like a prisoner. "Wait here!" Cleaners arrived with buckets and mops and disappeared into the girls' toilets.

Miss Bruce came back out and glared at me. "I might have guessed. Charcoal has been found. What do you have to say for yourself?"

I mustn't giggle.

"Sorree, Miss Bruce." I pulled in my cheeks to make my face serious. But it sounded so stupid. *Charcoal has been found.*

She stood there glaring at me. "You have lied and you have blocked a toilet and it is lucky for you that the caretakers have managed to unblock it before it flooded the education centre. Otherwise your parents would be receiving a bill for several hundred pounds."

I nodded.

A seagull squawked just outside the doors. Miss Bruce ducked. "Eugh!"

She breathed in loudly. Her face went calm again. "Well, you will miss the games evening. You can sit on your own, Maya Sheridan, and think about your behaviour."

Rose:
A Bottle

I wish you'd talk to me, Maya. Why can't you talk to me?

My sketchbook was filling up.

My head kept pounding. The education centre was too full of noise.

Maya was getting in trouble all the time.

I kept working, slowly finishing the spines of the thistle, then I sketched a blue bottle from the beach.

When Grandma paints she forgets everything, she says. I rubbed my finger down the cloudy glass with its flecks and scratches. I wondered if it used to have a drink in it or a chemical. The glass was very thick. If it was mine, I would put a cork in it and a message inside like people used to. When it was in the sea maybe it was so exactly sea-coloured you wouldn't see it until it washed up.

The teachers were all looking at Maya and talking about her. I should never have told Clemmy anything about us. About home. I should never have let Clemmy run to get Miss Bruce in the night.

Mum had asked me to keep an eye on Maya and I had got her into more trouble instead.

I mixed greens and blues and softly filled in the

shape of the bottle, blending the colours.

"Your sister's getting worse," Clemmy said. "And I'm not talking to you, Rose."

Maya:
Moods

Before dinner we were all supposed to choose three objects to draw from the big smelly collection, or write in our trip diaries, or write a postcard home. Boring!

I sat on my own again and drew my perfectly round stone cos that was just drawing a ball. I drew my bit of charcoal and coloured it in completely black. Some of the charcoal got rubbed a bit on my arm, so my picture was quite smudgy. Next I started drawing Georgie's starfish. Its legs were so odd; they didn't seem to fit its body in my drawing. They looked like spiders' legs, falling off. My sketches were rubbish basically.

Bonnie called, "Maya, come and help me!" She had hardly started her drawing, so I drew my perfectly round stone on her paper and we drew a little person coming out of a door in the side of it.

Clemmy was up at the front asking Miss Stewart lots of questions about the sea because she wanted to look clever and interested.

Rose was sitting hunched over, sketching. I didn't want to even see her picture. But I did go past, just once, and the bottle sketch was all right,

I suppose. I mean, it wasn't a very difficult shape. Anyone could have drawn it really.

She must have thought she looked like a proper artist, showing off with her handful of different colours and her special little brush for blending. She turned away from me with a blank face and I thought, *Wouldn't it be great if something very wet dropped on her picture?* I could rush into the toilets and bring back dripping toilet paper and throw it on the carefully blended blue to make blue soup.

But I didn't do it.

I wandered outside and found all my Cormorants team staring in the window of the Whitesands shop, where hoodies were hanging up. I joined them very quietly, but Dillon saw me. "I bet the winners get to choose which colour they want," he said. "Not talking to you, Maya Sheridan." And he walked away.

The dome shape of the island wasn't a human head with standing-up hair, at least not the way they did it on the sweatshirt. It was the head of a seal, with added whiskers. It was surrounded by sea. And it had huge eyes.

"I'd have purple," I said, staring at the seal.

But, when I turned round, all my friends had gone.

I missed the games evening. It looked rubbish anyway – dodgeball and stuff with hoops. I got one of my secret packets of sweets out of my suitcase. I was supposed to sit inside but I sneaked out and talked to the seagulls. There were so many flying around this place. I loved the noise they made. Everyone said they were a pest and not to feed them. But I loved to watch them. Plus, one of them looked exactly like the one I saw on the first morning. He was especially tame and came right up to me. He had a darker patch on one wing. I decided to call him Gordon. He liked chocolate swirls.

Miss Bruce made my life ten times worse because when we were going to bed she said, "Letting people down today. Letting yourself down. You should be proud to have such a gifted sister. Not all of us can excel, but doing your best means you can face yourself at the end of the day." Then she put her toothbrush back in her mouth and I couldn't hear the rest.

I do do my best, I thought, *you horrid hairclip woman. And I'm stuck in here while Rose gets to lie in her comfy cabin with her friends.*

When a person is bad, mostly they just get worse. Rose just gets better and better. Maybe one day there will be a Rose medal just for Roseness. I bet she was laughing her socks off about me. I bet she and Clemmy were laughing enough to burst.

I wished I could put Rose and Miss Bruce and Clemmy in a marooned boat far out to sea, and they would have to starve until seagulls found them and ate them because there wouldn't be any islands near enough, and the seagulls would be swooping and swooping...

I smiled to myself, turned over and fell asleep.

Rose:
Leaps

"Don't look down. One step at a time, Rose," he said.

It was next morning and we all stood around the Leap of Faith. Alex, the instructor, showed us how the harness was fitted and we all looked at a brown pole that went up and up, with footrests on either side, a tower on the top and a swing to grab. Miss Bruce said each person who did it right would get ten points for their team.

The Leap of Faith was the jump. The faith was being brave and letting go as you reached to catch the bar. I saw it on the Whitesands film trailer before we came. After this we would all be allowed to do the Treetops walkways.

I was one of the first to go. The pole felt taller and wider now I was near it. Climbing up the footrests wasn't too hard.

All those faces staring up at me.

"Don't look down," Mr Goodman called.

As I got higher the pole made little creaking sounds. Could it fall? No, I thought, Whitesands had been here for ten years; the pole had never fallen over. Getting my leg over the top to stand on the platform was hard and the pole actually swayed. People shouted up, "You can do it, Rose!"

When we do parallel bars and I'm on the top one, I feel as if the world has dropped down, but also like it's racing up to meet me. There's a horrible high-up feeling.

The bar looked so far out of reach. Surely no one could catch that. I stood there on the platform wobbling. My arms felt thin and short. So much sky between me and that length of swinging metal. There would be a moment where there was just me flying before I caught it… I stretched and stretched right on tiptoes, further … further… My feet bounced. I dropped, grabbed, catching the swing, the harness jerking me up, yanking my arms. I sailed down, gripping the cool bar, my legs swinging backwards and forwards.

On the ground again I hugged my arms to myself and everyone clapped and said well done. I blushed and rushed away into the crowd.

Clemmy set off up the pole next. I squinted at the orange bottom of her trainers. She climbed in a beautiful neat monkey way. She reached out for the swing, launched herself out and grabbed it, swung and got lowered down.

"It's a great view," she told everyone, pointing her toes and doing a little bow as she landed. "And too easy really."

Next came Maya's friend Jake. We all cheered him on. He's much bigger than Clemmy and he kept missing the footrests and calling "whoops!" and everyone was mimicking him, until Miss Bruce shouted, "Be quiet!"

"Now, guys, we should help people to make their leap and not make fun of them," Mr Goodman said, staring up at Jake's legs.

As he reached out to catch the swing Jake called out, "My trousers have ripped," and everyone laughed again.

"Are you going to do it too, Mr Goodman?" Georgie asked.

"I can't ask you all to be brave and not be brave myself, can I?" Mr Goodman said.

So he went up the pole next. His legs were so long it was really quick; he seemed to do it all in about three shunts. I caught the flash of him leaping, then he was back down at the bottom again and we were all clapping and whooping. It's good if teachers are brave.

"Your turn, Miss Bruce?" Bonnie said.

"I won't be climbing the pole," Miss Bruce replied.

We all went quiet. Miss Bruce going up the pole was a terrible idea.

"Why?" Bonnie asked.

We waited.

"Well, Bonnie, I suffer from vertigo," Miss Bruce said sternly.

"Can vertigo people not climb?" Bonnie asked.

"No, they can't, Bonnie," Miss Stewart said. "They don't like being high up."

"Who is going next?" snapped Miss Bruce.

Bonnie wanted to go up the pole. They let her try going a little way up in the harness with Miss Stewart on the other side and then made her come down again.

Next it was Maya.

"Now, are you definitely going to be all right with this, Maya?" Mr Goodman asked. "How is your leg feeling?"

"My leg's fine. I want to do it. I can," I heard her say.

They clipped on the harness and she put on the yellow helmet.

She pawed the ground by the pole. "It's like three houses tall!" she called.

Clemmy grabbed my arm. "Let's not watch. Let's

practise our routine. Everyone's so busy watching Maya, they won't care what we do." She yanked my arm. "Come on!"

"No, wait," I said.

Maya hoisted herself up the first few steps, waved down. "Ah-ee-ah-ee-ah!" She turned into Tarzan. Everyone was laughing, of course.

Clemmy huffed. "She can't do it elegantly. That's why she's being a gorilla or whatever it is."

"You-hoo-hoo. I wanna be like you-oo-oo!" Maya sang. She laughed. "I'm going so high, I'll touch the sky!"

She was past halfway.

Miss Bruce stood with her hands on her hips and her cross face. "Save the silly behaviour. No one is impressed."

Maya wiggled and jiggled. She squealed an odd high squeal. Her legs bicycled.

Everyone giggled more.

Now she was grabbing at the pole as if it had gone slippery, her legs kicking. I caught my breath.

And then she just fell off.

The harness hooked her up like a puppet. One of the instructors shouted, "Grip the pole!" but Maya swung back, hanging there in the air, calling,

"No!" and waving her arms and legs around.

"Bring her down!" snapped Miss Bruce.

Maya sailed to the ground and people clustered around her.

I craned to see her through the crowd. I felt cold. My head pounded. Why had she fallen off?

"She flunked it. What was the point of that? It wasn't even funny," Clemmy said. "Just per-thetic."

"She wanted to do the leap," I said. "Why didn't she carry on?"

"Showing off is completely like Maya. She's immature," Clemmy said.

"I don't mean the showing off. She seemed to fall, really fall." I wished I could see her. Why couldn't I see her?

"She just wanted to muck about. They won't give her another go," Clemmy said.

Maya always loved jumping. And that odd squeal. Something else was wrong.

Maya:
Activity Day

Twang … twang… My leg felt terrible!

Mr Goodman was looking down at me. "Are you all right, Maya?"

I sat up. "It was a laugh," I said, making a joking face. I rubbed my eyes quickly with the back of my hand. "I changed my mind. The pole was … quite boring."

Shut up, leg. Leave me alone. I hate you, leg. You are the worst leg in the world.

"Is your leg bothering you? Mrs Olson could have a quick look."

"No!"

Mr Goodman's face flickered with different moods, like Dad. "In that case I'm disappointed," he said. "You and I had better have a chat later." And he just went away.

Dillon was the next one looking down at me, his face all thundery. "Why did you do that? That's ten points you lost us!"

"It was a laugh," I said again, holding my ankle between my hands, fires flashing under my fingers.

Why did you have to turn to jelly? You are no good at being a leg.

"Don't worry, I'll do the next bit properly," I

said.

"No, you won't. You're always showing off. You just don't care. Well, you're rubbish. I don't want you." Dillon walked away.

Georgie appeared. "Oh, Maya. The teachers were really cross. Miss Bruce said you were an attention seeker. You were so wiggly and jumpy, showing off like that…"

I pressed the sides of my ankle. *Stop … please stop.*

My leg was shouting louder than Georgie talking.

"What will you do now? Just sit and watch, I suppose. Maybe you could offer to do scoring. I'm going on the Treetops course."

Mum used to tell me to give the pain a number, when I was having physio. This was a nine out of ten. It hadn't felt this bad for ages, not for months. I gulped. I wanted Mum … Gran … home.

Nobody was near me now. They were all cheering for the next person climbing the pole.

The first day Rose won something without me, Gran and Grandad went to watch. It was a secret plan that they had all made and not told me about. I was at the hospital with Mum and

Lisa and Rob, the physios, arm rails either side of me like the travelator at the airport, being told I was supposed to walk from one end to the other. Every time I stood, Stupid Leg collapsed, over and over and over. Lisa and Rob said, "You can do this, Maya." But it wasn't about *me* doing it; it was Stupid Leg that wouldn't. And each time they said, "You can do it," it made me angrier and angrier until I exploded and folded into a bundle. "Shut up! My leg is useless. It won't do anything."

Just now, on that pole, it was the same.

Miss Bruce had left her register behind. I got up and limped slowly to the bench.

I opened the shiny red folder. Points and scores. And by each name little comments. Things like, *Blonde with glasses.* I looked down the list. Maya Sheridan. *Brown, short, shows off. Annoying.*

A wave of fury filled me up.

I took her pen from the clip on the side. *Hilary Bruce*, I wrote at the bottom of the list, then next to it, *Bossy and scared of poles.*

My friends thought I was useless. The teachers thought I was useless. I'd ruined everything. I couldn't even climb a pole. And all because of Stupid Leg.

The teams up in the trees were shrieking alongside the *zuzz* of the zip wire. People were calling, "Quick… Hold on…! *Wheee!*"

That used to be one of my favourite things. Now all I could do was shuffle along.

Shut up, Stupid Leg!

Bonnie was with Miss Stewart on the boring-people bench.

She came over. "Don't talk to me. I've gone invisible," I said.

Her mouth wobbled and she stood still. "Can't I even…?"

"No!" I held up my hand. "No one can talk to invisible people."

"Are you bored, Maya, sweetheart?" Miss Stewart called. "Maybe you should sit down for a while. I'm looking after the waifs and strays. Hassan's got a tummy ache and Bonnie is going to play a game."

Why would I join in with that? Games like that are for tiny children who can hardly even speak.

I was good with my arms. I was good at throwing.

"Can I go back to the cabins and get my water bottle?" I asked.

"Of course." Miss Stewart smiled. "Come

straight back."

I set off.

Mum's voice sounded in my head, saying, "Maya, love, there's no need to be rude. Rob and Lisa are trying to help."

"Well, they aren't," I remember screaming. "I'll live downstairs. I'll use the frame. I don't need to walk. Just go away all of you. Go away!"

Through the trees to the cabins. Not so far. *Shut up, leg.* I clenched my fists. *Shut up!*

When one of Rose's gym events was going to happen, all my family secretly agreed who was going to go to it and take photos for the others. They would stop talking when I came into a room. When I checked Mum's phone there was Rose, upside-down cartwheeling, stretching, toes touching her nose like a really stupid folded thing.

Now I opened the door of Rose's cabin and found her Tumblers bag on her bed.

You may be the runner, but my arms are strong enough for anything!

I liked the green and blue stripes. I took the bag outside, held on to the straps and started to spin.

I was having my own activity day!

Rose:
Treetops

From my high place on a platform I saw Maya going away through the trees.

She was limping badly, almost dragging her leg. She didn't know I was watching her. She couldn't be pretending. She must really be in pain.

Should I go and find her? I stared up into the leaves. No. She would be horrible. I was the last person she wanted.

Tell a teacher? No. She would just get in more trouble.

"Do you want to go next, Rose?" Marcus asked.

I stared along the zip wire, blinking back tears.

Maybe you will feel better quickly, Maya. Maybe you just banged it.

"Yes," I heard myself say softly.

Suddenly I was clipping myself on and hurtling down along the wire through the trees, wobbling on the rubber seat. "*Wheee!*" The wind whooshed by me. I half fell off at the end, laughing, spinning round.

"I'm doing it again!" I shouted, dragging the seat back to give Marcus a turn.

I had another turn and then another. Me and Marcus didn't talk, just took turns to push each other to get going.

I went faster and faster. Doing the zip wire made everything else go away. Plus, I wasn't with Clemmy. Or Maya. Nobody was making me do ANYTHING.

Clemmy was waiting for me at the end of the course. "Why did you take so long?" she asked.

"I just … I love the zip wire," I said.

Clemmy's face had a closed-up look. "We won't have time for the exercises I was planning. You are very disappointing."

Maya:
New Bird
Feeder

I eased Miss Bruce's door shut, waves of horrified excitement rushing through me. She'd called me an attention seeker. She'd said I was annoying.

The bins behind the cafeteria were great big blue ones, like the ones at school. I collected thrown-away bread … egg … potato … bacon.

I filled up the food holders in my special new bird feeder and hooked it over the beam outside the cabin.

Jake found me in the trees, watching. "Everyone's on their way back," he said, and then, "Maya, what are you doing?"

"An experiment," I said.

It was like a scary film. *Bdum … bdum … bdum … * pulsing in my head.

My class flooded through the trees and the teachers came too, busy in conversation. Seagulls wheeled in the sky, saw the food, dive-bombed. The air filled with squawks. Everyone rushed to watch the feeding frenzy. I couldn't stop shuddering and giggling. They dived to get their special dinner so fast Miss Bruce nearly missed seeing it. The swinging bra was empty in about ten seconds flat. I should have filled it up more.

Miss Bruce yelled, "Who did this?", roaring

like a giant. She ran back towards the Treetops walkways.

Jake wasn't smiling. He was just staring at me with a cold face. "She was really upset," he said.

"She's always bossing me," I said. "It was a laugh."

"I think it was mean."

"She's mean to me," I said.

"She's just trying to be a teacher, Maya."

My mouth fell open. "Don't be stupid," I said.

"I'm fed up with you always calling me stupid," Jake said. "I hate it. You've turned horrible, Maya. Someone should tell you. You didn't use to be like this. You're not my friend any more."

Rose:
The Lost
Bag

Clemmy and I stared up at my Tumblers bag high up on our cabin roof. "How did *that* get up *there*? It was *her*, wasn't it? Well, that does it. I'm going to get a teacher."

"No, please…" I began. But I wanted my bag.

"You have to stop being so stupid, Rose!" Clemmy flounced away.

The weather forecast said there might be rain later on. My bag had all my things inside it, unless the zip had come undone and they'd fallen out. But I couldn't see anything – just my bag with its straps thrown wide. I thought of my sketchbook and pencil case, my special little binoculars, my watercolour paints, my locker key and lanyard, my mints, my water bottle, my gloves.

Where was Maya? She must have been OK if she threw the bag … but I had seen her limping. Clemmy just wanted her to be in trouble. I couldn't get her into more trouble. That would be such a mean thing to do.

I heard voices and Clemmy came back with Mr Goodman.

"It looks a nice bag, Rose. How did it get up there?" he said.

"I don't know," I said.

"Well, it looks like someone threw it, doesn't it?"

I looked down at the ground, feeling my face go scarlet.

All in a rush Clemmy began talking, not even stopping to breathe. "Rose won't tell you, but I will. It wasn't a game. It's her sister Maya. She does horrible things all the time. She threw an egg at Rose the day they were leaving. She might throw anything. She might throw something at you, Mr Goodman. She's completely out of control and Rose never tells on her and she's getting worse, and—"

Mr Goodman ran his hand through his curly hair and walked round to the back of the cabin to stare at my bag. "Clemmy," he called, appearing at the other side, "Rose might rather talk to me herself?"

"She won't." Clemmy gave me a meaningful look. "Maya put a plant in Rose's boot."

"When was this?"

"The first day. The Sensory Trail. She actually stole Rose's boot and vandalised it. And the crab, that was her too. And now this! You never fight back, do you, Rose?"

Mr Goodman folded his arms. "Thank you for

your help. I think I'd like to talk to Rose on my own now."

"What you have to understand is Maya is seriously trying to ruin Rose's life and she's actually doing it."

Mr Goodman sighed. "You've been a big help and now I'd like you to go and find the rest of the group. Could you do that, Clemmy?"

"I think it would be better for me to wait for Rose."

"No! That's not better!" I shouted, my voice so loud that Clemmy and Mr Goodman both sort of jumped. Mr Goodman's eyebrows shot up. Words came out of my mouth. "Stop bossing me, Clemmy. You just boss me. You've made me have a headache. Go and find the others like Mr Goodman said. Just go!"

Mr Goodman's eyebrows stayed high.

"Well!" Clemmy did a big angry huff and stomped away.

It felt very quiet without her.

Mr Goodman turned to me. I felt my face hot and flaming.

"Tell you what, let's sort this bag out," he said. "You and I don't know each other very well, do we, Rose? But if there's something you should tell me… Well, don't carry around lots of worries on your own." Mr Goodman moved a window box then went away and came back with a long brush. He clambered up on to the ledge. "You don't always have to protect your sister, you know."

I started to cry.

Maya:
The Brave
Interesting Girl

More telling off!

"I thought the bra would dry better in the sun," I said.

Mr Goodman was looking very hard at me. "Maya, can you explain why we found your sister's bag on the roof of her cabin?"

Stupid Leg twanged. Like a guitar. I was turning into a musical instrument. The twanging went on and on.

I looked down at the grass. Green things. I made a list. Apple shampoo. My towel with the waving worms on it. A green Halloween wig. Was green my favourite colour after red? No, yellow was.

I nodded. Then shook my head. I'd forgotten the question.

"On this trip you seem like a different person, Maya," Mr Goodman said.

I felt my lips go tight. I kept my eyes down, studying the grass...

"Do you need to have a chat with Mrs Olson about your leg? Is it hurting?"

I shook my head.

Twang ... twang ... twang.

"You seem to be in a bad mood with everyone,

even your friends. You don't seem to be your best self." Mr Goodman had a nice voice.

You're wrong, I thought, *this is me. I've turned horrible. Jake said so.*

Mr Goodman was looking at me – really looking – and waiting. "Do you know, when you first came back into school after your surgery, you were a person that I really admired?" he said. "Where has that brave, interesting girl gone?"

Tears came into my eyes. I rubbed them away. *I don't know*, I thought. *That girl went away. She was only interesting when she could run and leap and* be someone.

Mr Goodman looked busy again. He sighed, zipping up his fleece. "Well, I will not have this trip ruined, by you or by anyone. And I think you are letting everyone down. But most of all, you're letting yourself down."

He didn't care.

Rose:
Not Listening

We sat in the cafeteria drinking orange squash and eating bananas. My head was pounding. I'd checked inside my Tumblers bag and everything was there. But now Mr Goodman knew. Maybe he would ring Mum and Dad and Maya would get into more and more trouble. She might even get sent home.

"You need to explain more about your sister, how bad she is," Clemmy said through bits of banana. She wagged her finger at me.

"And you're not doing enough training, *and* Mum said you were only borderline for the squad... Do you know what borderline means? I'm actually getting cross now, Rose."

Clemmy was a mouth, always complaining.

I closed my eyes. Opened them.

"The whole point in having a schedule is to..."

Closed them.

Something's happening to you, Maya, isn't it? And it's getting worse.

I opened my eyes.

"Are you listening to me at all, Rose Sheridan?"

"No," I said.

Maya:
Get Well
Soon

"We're all going to play Frisbee," Mr Goodman said, leading us down to the beach. "And, by the way, Miss Bruce has gone to lie down. I'd like you all to think hard about that. She joined us on this trip out of kindness."

My class all made shapes in the air, like dancers, trying to get the Frisbee. Jake and Dillon ran, leaped and pulled each other over. Mr Goodman was so tall. Miss Stewart could run really fast. Voices carried across the sand. Everyone seemed so happy. Three Frisbees were flying and soaring with people dashing after them.

I walked slowly to a rock, sat down and stared out at the island. The sea sometimes looks happy when you are on holiday, but other times it makes you sadder. I looked for my seal, but he hadn't come out to play this afternoon.

Twang twang from my leg.

Seals wouldn't play Frisbee. If they did, they'd be best at catching it on their noses. Could the seals see me? Were they looking for me too?

"I don't think it's going to be possible to live," I remember saying after the accident and Gran said, "Don't say that; don't ever say that."

I thought about Dolphin Ward: the sticky

plastic sheet on the bed, not wanting to look at my leg, not being able to walk to the toilet, people treating me as if I was little, the smell of all the hospital cleaning things, nurses coming and going, Grandad coming to see me, calling me a poor lass and going away. I remembered looking out of the window at the black gnarly tree and the car park and the cars moving in and out, and thinking where were all those cars going, and maybe one of them was going to our road?

I remembered Doctor Chance discussing me and holding X-rays, showing me the pins. "Not like drawing pins," he said. "But the bone is not fusing, not really knitting together as much as we would like... We might need to explore again."

And me saying, "No, don't explore it again!"

Dr Chance said, "Sometimes we talk about a new kind of normal, where things are never going to be exactly the same, but will still get much better. Do you understand? If you get more pain, that's a sign that we need to adjust as you grow."

They would make me have another operation. That's what this pain meant.

I remembered the stupid sandal Mum brought for me that was big as a boat.

And the first time Mum brought Rose. She was in her Tumblers hoodie, her tracksuit, her trainers, standing at the window.

"Everyone at school says hi." She stood on tiptoes, then on one leg. "They made you a card." She handed it to me. "Get well soon."

I wanted my own hoodie with Tumblers on.

Could the seals see me now? They must be watching, mustn't they?

I remembered going back to school after my accident: my wheelchair, people gathering around me, the disabled toilet by the office, and everyone staring at assembly. I remembered Archie and Dillon spinning me until the playground supervisor said, "No, you can't do that – she'll fall out," and them running off and away. I remembered the teaching assistant forgetting to collect me when the bell went and leaving me stranded by the apparatus, and the teacher coming to get me herself, my crutches with the stickers on, bumping up the stairs to my bedroom on my bum, wearing the carpet thin. The red and green sprinkles and glitter on my smelly plaster, the showers with a bag on my leg, and shouting for things because everything was in the wrong place.

Gran said that animals could sense when people needed them, like maybe if a person was in pain, a dog would lie beside them and lick their face. Animals were better than people.

Wasn't that a bobbing shape, just out where the sheen of the water was pure silver?

Jake was right: I had turned horrible. My friends weren't my friends any more. They were racing along the beach in the fading light and leaping and calling.

I could just imagine the doctor. "There will be more surgery. Inevitable, I'm afraid."

At dinnertime no one was speaking to me. Dillon sat there laughing with Jake. Archie was all sad and quiet, and Georgie just giggled with Ellie. On the teacher table they all chatted, except for Miss Bruce, who didn't come for any food at all. I think Miss Stewart was telling a joke because they were all laughing.

We ate a strange chicken pie, and I made the pie into the island and the potatoes and peas into the sea. Then Miss Stewart called out, "OK, everyone, listening please. There's something I want to show you. Look at this terrific work. Rose Sheridan, stand up so everyone can see you. This is Rose's trip sketchbook. You've done this very detailed drawing of a crab. This must have taken you ages. Wonderful thistle from the dunes. Glass bottle – such a lovely blue." Everyone clapped and whooped.

"Well deserved," Miss Stewart said. "I'm going to leave Rose's sketchbook out, so everyone can have a look through it. Exceptional."

Everyone thought she was brilliant. Rose was the cleverest, best, brightest thing.

I couldn't be here any more. I didn't belong here. I wasn't good at anything.

I didn't care about the Talent Show, but everyone else couldn't wait to go and practise.

"You can have half an hour," said Mr Goodman. "I'm very excited to see all these talents."

Some people didn't mind practising in the cafeteria, but Ellie said, "We don't want everyone to see us before the show."

"OK," Mr Goodman said, smiling. "I can understand if you want it to be a surprise. How about you use cabins, the cafeteria, the Hang-Out? As long as you wear your coats. When you hear the bell we need everyone back, so we can start promptly at seven thirty."

We flooded out.

Miss Stewart rushed past me. She was making an awful noise, sort of gulping. "I'm going to be sick," she said.

Mrs Olson had her arm round Miss Stewart's shoulder. "Miss Stewart isn't very well," she called. "Maya, you and Bonnie can practise for the show together, can't you?" She pushed open the doors of the ladies' loo.

"No," I said.

"Yes," said Bonnie, appearing behind me.

The loo door shut.

"Is Miss Stewart ill?" Bonnie asked. She grinned, all fun and laughing. "What are we practising?"

"We're not." I swung past her, out and down the path to the cabins.

Shut up, leg.

I flung open my cabin door. I only wanted my warm fleece that Gran gave me, the one she calls my "baby sheep". I dropped a bag of chocolate stars into the pocket. The door flew open. Bonnie again.

"I'm not practising for the show, Bonnie," I said. "Find someone else."

Bonnie watched me pulling the fleece on.

"Where are you going?" she asked.

"Away." I slid past her.

She picked up her pink bag from her own bed. "Can I come?"

"No."

We crossed the Hang-Out. All around us people were getting ready. A heavy beat began blasting out from one of the summerhouses. Someone rushed past across the grass in a pink wig.

I speeded up. *Shut up, leg!*

A lorry was parked by the kitchens and the gates were open. I was off, down the slope towards the sea. Bonnie waved her stupid pink bag.

Suddenly I didn't care. "Do what you want."

She grabbed my arm. "I can help you."

A funny surge happened inside me. "I'll tell you a secret. I'm going forever."

Bonnie laughed. "That's OK. I've brought my emergency handbag!"

Rose:
Concentrating

Everyone clapped when Miss Stewart said well done for the sketchbook and I stood there, my face all red. When I sat down Clemmy said, "I bet our team will get extra points for that."

I didn't look at Maya.

They passed round the chocolate brownies and I nibbled at one.

Mr Goodman said, "You can all have half an hour to practise for the Talent Show. I know some of you have brought music and things. I've actually brought my guitar, so I'll be practising too."

People took extra brownies because no one moved the tray up the table and I think the kitchen people had gone to clear up.

Clemmy and me waited until there was space in the cafeteria to practise our routine, which meant watching everyone pile out and pushing some tables away to clear a space.

"We're losing precious time," Clemmy said.

There were some blue mats on a rack and we dragged four down and started warming up and stretching.

I had an odd feeling in my stomach. I wished I hadn't eaten the chocolate brownie. The dizzy headache settled over my eyes again. I didn't want to do the routine, all the tumbling and balances. Where was Maya? Where had she gone? What would she practise?

"I actually think they should give you and me extra time to perform," Clemmy said, flipping into a handstand. "Our routine lasts more than five minutes and some people will just be singing along to a song or something..." I held her legs. "Concentrate, Rose."

"Yeah. Sorry."

But then the cafeteria door flew open and Mrs Olson appeared. She was panting, as if she'd been running. "Have you girls seen Bonnie?"

"No," Clemmy said, and then, turning to me: "Right, Rose, let's get started."

A wave of worry hit me. I let go of Clemmy's legs and she flopped down. "But what about Miss Stewart...?"

"She's not feeling very well, unfortunately." Mrs Olson shook her head. "Could be a bug; hard to say at this stage. Please, if you do see Bonnie or Maya..." Her eyes had a wild sort of look.

"Aren't they in the cabins?" I asked.

Clemmy huffed. "We haven't seen them."

"I've checked the cabins and the Hang-Out."

Mrs Olson looked pleadingly at me. "I told them to practise together. I can't think where else to try."

"I'll … I'll tell them to come and find you in the Hang-Out, if I see them," I said.

"Thank you." The cafeteria door closed behind her.

Clemmy got into her opening pose, arms reaching out, front foot pointed. "Ready … three … two … one."

"No," I said. "I can't. I have to find them." I pulled on my boots.

"This is the limit, Rose Sheridan," Clemmy said. "And there is absolutely no way I am going to let you—"

But I didn't wait to hear the rest. I threw my rucksack over my shoulder and ran out of the door.

I ran into Maya's cabin first.

Her fleece was gone. And there was no sign of Bonnie's bag.

Where are you?

Are you all right?

I grabbed my mini binoculars and trained them first on the beach path, and then swept them around.

The causeway, that path out to Seal Island, had

two blurred shapes on it. Something sparkled –
Bonnie's purple jacket. My breath stopped.

I leaped for the door.

I ducked under the windows of the cafeteria as I
rushed past, so I didn't see Clemmy's furious face.

I'd get them to come back. I had to help Maya.
This time.

Maya:
Welcome
Home

A seal doesn't have bones in its tail. I'd like a tail like that; I could swap it for my legs. Seals were friendly and so was I. Seals liked being in groups. Seals didn't go to school.

It was harder to cross the causeway this time because there wasn't so much path, and I couldn't see the rocks nearly so well because it was getting dark and I'd forgotten my torch. Bonnie was useless at finding places for her feet and she kept moaning. But the island was getting bigger.

"I can hear the sea everywhere," Bonnie said, clambering over a big rock. "It's a long way. These rocks are so scratchy. I'm cold."

"You wanted to come," I said. "We're nearly there now."

"What will we do when we get there?"

"The seals will come and collect me. They'll bring my Selkie tail."

Bonnie gasped. "Really?"

"We just have to whistle," I said. "Do a big whistle and they'll hear."

"I can't whistle. Will they still want me if I can't whistle?" Bonnie asked.

"Blow." I pursed my lips together, like a kiss, to show her.

"The sea is whispering," I said. "Can you hear it?"

"Yes." Bonnie pulled herself up on to a big spiky rock and felt for the next one.

"They must be getting ready. They'll say welcome home," I said.

We clambered off the causeway to stare at our island.

"Come on, seals! Come out!" Bonnie called. "Are they in bed?" She danced away across the sand. "Make them come out, Maya."

We made our way along the little beach. There were big rocks standing out in the sea, making little islands, and Bonnie went *leap wobble leap wobble* out on to a rock, like a busy mermaid. I whistled. The noise came out a bit blowy. I tried again. This time it was clear and sharp.

I spotted a smooth head like a wet stone, a pair of bright seal eyes and a wide smiling mouth.

My heart soared – here they were. "Hooray!" we called.

My seal danced and bobbed in the water.

"Have you come to collect us?" I pulled off my boots and socks and clambered out on to the nearest rock.

Two more seals bobbed up near me. They flipped and danced.

I thought of the water therapy centre in hospital, my leg lifting and floating and all the pain stopping.

Bonnie peered down from her rock into the water. "It's like whirlpools, Maya."

I dangled my leg down. "Yeah, it's like whirlpools. Ooh!" I couldn't help gasping. The water in the therapy centre was like a warm bath, but this was freezing. I blinked back some tears. I swished my legs back and forward. The pain was still strong. But my leg would feel better soon. The seals would help me. They'd swim up and they'd help me. It was only the beginning. That was why my leg was still hurting.

Then I heard a voice from the causeway. I looked up. A figure was coming along the sand towards me.

"Maya. Bonnie. I found you."

Rose had come to ruin everything.

Rose:
Sea Rising

Maya stood on the little beach right by the water's edge. Her eyes flashed. "Go away, Rose. We don't want you!"

Bonnie was sitting on a rock sticking out of the sea further away from me, trailing her legs over the water.

"Just go away and win something, Rose!" Maya yelled.

"Yeah. Go away!" Bonnie yelled too.

I stared behind me at the mounting water. "Maya, you both have to come back," I pointed at the causeway. "The tide's coming in."

Maya glared. "Oh, the poor little causeway!"

I had to make her understand. "I checked at the coastguard's hut. We might be too late. We'll be stuck," I said.

She glared at me. "Who cares? Anyway, we're going to live here."

What was she talking about? My ears roared with the sound of the waves.

"Bonnie's not even allowed," I said desperately.

"The water's so cold, Maya," Bonnie called.

"Go away, Rose!" Maya splashed water at me.

"Why are you always so horrible?" I gasped,

freezing-cold water running down my face and hair.

Maya splashed again. "You got me put with a teacher! Go and tell on me again! Do a cartwheel. That's all you do, showing off all the time."

"I can't feel my legs," Bonnie called.

"I didn't. I never told. I wanted to, but I didn't!"

"You're always perfect, Rose," Maya said with a face of hate. "I'm sick of you!"

The sea roared. Every second it was flooding the causeway, drowning all the rock pools. I had to make her listen. "I'm not perfect. Nobody is. But you can't just stay here – it's not safe!"

Maya's face turned mocking. "Oooh, scared, are you?"

I could see Bonnie doing long sweeps of the water with her fingers. "I can't see the seals any more," she called. "Will our tails be warm?"

Why did my sister hate me so much?

"M-M-Maya, w-w-will the tails be warm? Please, Maya…" Bonnie called.

Maya made a smug kind of smile. "Bonnie and me are Selkies, Rose. The seals are bringing us tails."

"Is that what you're telling her?" Fury boiled

up inside me. "That's complete rubbish. You're making it up."

"M-M-Maya, I can't feel my legs," Bonnie bleated. "Are they coming? There's lots of sea, Maya. It's swirly. Why have the seals gone away?"

She leaned out over the water.

I gasped. "Maya, look at her!"

Bonnie yelped and slipped off the rock into the sea.

Maya:
Rescuing a Penguin

The furry hood of Bonnie's purple jacket fanned out like a sea anemone.

Rose froze in place, eyes huge with terror.

I had to get Bonnie.

I leaped from my rock down into the water. A wall of cold froze my legs. I gasped and half swam, half bounded towards Bonnie. Numbness filled me, but my arms thrashed. I reached the jacket. Dipped down. A big wave carried me off to a new place. No! I struggled back to the purple, rippling under the water. My legs were ice-pain, bicycling to nowhere. I dived again. I saw the hood, drifting, Bonnie's blonde hair streaming out. I threw my arms round her, clutching her to me, hauling her in. She was a huge lump. My arms screamed. I leaped, trying to hold her up, lost my way, tripped and gasped, plunging under the water again.

Then, suddenly, there was Rose with the beach behind her, reaching out to me. I heaved Bonnie up and we turned into a staggering three as Bonnie kicked and spluttered between us and I fell over on sand and coughed, my useless legs still gripped in a giant ice fist.

For a second we just shook like survivors. Hot

then cold shivers ran up and down me as the water streamed off. I sank on to a rock, useless, and Rose said furiously, "We have to get her warm. And you. Help me get her clothes off."

My teeth chattered. The beach and Rose kept wobbling and changing shape.

Rose wrestled Bonnie out of her wet clothes. "Quick!" Rose was an angry teacher, fighting with the zip on Bonnie's bag, pulling out a onesie. "Come on!"

She yanked up a zip. Bonnie was in a furry penguin onesie, black with a white tummy and a yellow beak dangling over her eyes.

"It's horrible here. I want my mum!" Bonnie wailed.

"And you, Maya!" Rose opened her rucksack, shook out clothes, socks, binoculars. "Take your things off. You'll be ill. Get them off." She wrenched my arms out of my sleeves, pulled a fleece out and leggings. "And there's extra socks. I'll put them on Bonnie."

I blinked. My arms and legs felt so heavy. Everything was misty and dripping. I was like a baby. *Rose is right. Put the clothes on*, I told myself. *Must get warm. Wet things off.*

I rubbed my eyes. "We have to find shelter," Rose was saying. "We can't get back. We're stuck. Maya!"

"I don't like this place. It's not the seaside any more," Bonnie said.

I watched Rose pull another thing from her rucksack, her silver sheet from when Dad did the Marathon. There was nothing Rose didn't have. Maybe she even had a house in there. I thought of a mean thing, but I didn't say it out loud.

I stood up. "I ... I... What do we do now?"

She wrapped the silver sheet round Bonnie's shoulders. I remembered when we met Dad at the end of the race and he was collapsing and grinning and we all wrapped ourselves up in the sheet and got the picture that's on the fridge. Thinking of Dad and Bonnie and everything, I started to cry.

"You saved her. You saved her, Maya," Rose said, and her voice was kind for the first time.

I kept wobbling, but I didn't fall. I saved Bonnie. I did, didn't I?

Rose:
The Wrong
Cave

Bonnie shivered and shook and clung to Maya, whining, "I want to go to bed. I want my mum."

Maya kept hugging her, saying, "I'm sorry. I'm sorry."

I kept thinking how my sister just dived in, straight into the water.

No one knew where we were. It was going to be night soon. No one would find us. The causeway was completely covered by the sea. The tiny lights of Whitesands glinted. But so far away.

You have to get people warm quickly if they've fallen in the sea. Maya was slow. I don't think she could think very well. I made Bonnie put on my extra walking socks on top of the onesie, and then my scarf, but she was still shaking, and she looked so weird in the furry suit, like a toddler. I led them slowly to the back of the island, to the caves. "Let's go in here," I said. "It will be warmer." The cave opening was an archway with a big rock in front. As we edged round it, I caught a flash of white inside.

"Eugh!" A smell wafted out like rotting dead horrible things, so bad it made me blink and choke.

"Look!" Bonnie cried.

At the back of the cave, there was a furry white

creature with dark marble eyes and the most beautiful face. It was like a puffball of white making a strange mewing noise. A baby seal, all on its own!

"Oooh!" Maya reached out to it.

And then, suddenly, there was a massive grey shining tower in the cave's entrance right beside us, barking and honking.

"Quick! Get out!" I shouted. "I think that's its mum!"

Maya grabbed Bonnie. The adult seal reared up, waggling its head, honking, waving its flippers and lurching towards me. "*Hooonk … hoooonk.*" The noise was massive, deafening.

"It'll crush us!" I shouted. I waved the silver blanket, whooshing it at the seal as Maya and Bonnie stumbled back round the rock.

"*Raaaooo,*" went the seal, still coming at me, dodging the blanket.

I leaped after the others and stumbled away from the cave. The sounds of honking droned on, but it was muffled now, deeper inside.

Maya and Bonnie clung together further up the beach.

"I want to go home. Take me home," Bonnie sobbed.

"That was close," Maya said. "That seal really hated us."

We had to be inside. We had to find a safe place.

I chose a smaller cave and got my torch out, and we sneaked in carefully, checking for angry seals. We stood for ages, staring out of the opening, scared to sit down.

Maya looked miserable now.

"Wasn't that seal huge?" Bonnie said.

"She thought her baby was in danger," I said.

"Maya, seals smell so bad," Bonnie said. "Do they all smell like that?" She curled up between us and laid her head across Maya's knees. "We can't live with them, Maya. I would be sick every day!"

"I'm turning my torch off. We might need it." I put the torch back in my rucksack and rubbed my hands together. The darkness seemed to close around us. The back of the cave was just a mass of black. The moon lit the sea in bands of light.

I kept replaying the noise the seal made, the big animal pain. "Mum made a noise like that when you were hurt in hospital. Sort of angry with everyone," I said.

Maya stared at me, quiet. I wrapped the silver blanket round us. I didn't feel properly warm exactly. Just a bit less freezing-cold. The silver blanket must be made of something really clever.

"How did you find us?" Maya asked me in a flat voice.

I breathed the heavy sea smell. "I saw you through Grandad's binoculars," I said. "I was worried."

Bonnie sighed, and her breathing went slow.

We made our voices soft, whispering. "Would the tide come all the way in here?" Maya asked.

"No. The rocks are dry," I said.

She played with a bit of Bonnie's hair, twisting it between her fingers. Bonnie looked so odd curled up, like a really little child going to bed.

"I'll be able to go for help when the tide goes out again. I'll run back," I said.

"It's easy for *you*," Maya said crossly. But then, "We're trapped all night, aren't we?"

"No one could cross the causeway in the dark. Even if the tide was out," I told her. "It's too dangerous. You could go the wrong way and fall in the sea."

It was so dark in the cave now; we were just a silver glinting hump. "Rose," Maya said softly, "I don't want you to go. Even when it's safe, I mean. I don't want to be here ... just me and Bonnie.

What if she… What if I…?"

I stared out at the sea. "I have to. I mean, I don't want to go either, but it's safer if I do."

I shivered. Bonnie shouldn't be here like this. We'd be in such trouble. No one would find us in a cave, would they? A sob came from my mouth.

"Shush," Maya said. "You'll wake her."

I made little gulps, staring at line upon line of moving light on the sea

"I miss you, Rose," Maya said.

"Maybe it won't take me very long to go back across, when it's light and—" I pictured scrambling back over the causeway.

"No," Maya said. "I meant I miss you. I miss you all the time. Every day I miss you."

A shock went through me. "Do you?"

Maya's head went down.

I sat in the dark. I don't know how long, but I just sat there watching Dad's silver blanket shaking.

"I'm cold." Bonnie stirred and shivered. "I want some hot chocolate."

I flicked the torch on again and our faces were lit up with rat's-tail hair and starey eyes. We looked like Halloween people, like zombies.

"I'm cold too," Maya said.

I pulled a bar of chocolate from my rucksack and broke off bits for all of us. Then we all had some water from my bottle. It was ice cold.

"That's it," I said. "Nothing else useful."

"My packet of chocolate stars fell in the sea," Maya said. "I didn't bring anything else."

"What shall we do now?" Bonnie asked. "Tell me a story. Do 'The Seal and the Butterfly' again."

"Once there was a seal and a butterfly…"

I watched Maya. She had this look, as if she was somewhere else. Her voice went softer. She must have told this story before. But I'd never heard it.

Bonnie wriggled happily. "And was the butterfly still showing off and the seal wishing she could fly? I liked when the seal rolled down the rock and everyone laughed."

"This is a new bit," Maya said. "One day the butterfly flew up to the seal, who was lounging on her favourite rock. And the butterfly said, 'I'm clever, I'm clever.' And she flapped her beautiful silky red and gold wings, and everyone was watching because she was such a beautiful butterfly and even the seal was watching, even though she was sick of her calling, 'I can fly, I can fly, I'm a brilliant butterfly.'"

Maya's eyes were lit up. She was making the story alive. Maya had a power.

"But then the butterfly didn't look where she was going, and she swooped low and a big wave caught her, *splash*, and pulled her under the water. And there was no one to help her because her only friend was miles away inside a flower. But the seal had seen what happened and she whumped off her rock, over the pebbles and dived into the sea. The butterfly was struggling, and her beautiful red and gold wings were soaked like wet newspaper all the way through to her neat, pointy legs. She dropped down and down into the deep blue water. 'Help!' she tried to call, but she was going to drown in the dark, dark sea."

Bonnie stiffened.

Maya's voice rose. "Suddenly, as her body drifted, something came underneath her, lifting her up and up, and the next thing she knew she was back in the bright daylight draped across the seal's nose like a little coloured hankie. The seal laid her on a rock to dry."

Bonnie breathed out loudly. "How long did it take?"

"Not long. Steam came off and she fluffed herself

up again and sat up and stretched her wings. 'You have saved my life and I will never, ever forget it.'"

Bonnie wriggled. "Did they cry?"

"Yes."

I stared at my sister. "I'm glad the butterfly was all right," I said.

Maya:
Let's Tell
Them

Bonnie yawned. "Can we go to bed soon?"

I thought about Miss Stewart always sitting beside Bonnie, guiding her hand for writing. "Nobody knows where we are, Bonnie," I said gently.

"Can't we tell them?" Bonnie said, uncurling a bit and stretching her arms.

Rose and me nodded to each other.

"Yes. I'm going to run back for some help when it's day," Rose said. "So it will all be fine, Bonnie."

Bonnie looked around. "I don't like this place. My bones are too cold."

I rubbed up and down her arm and shoulder. "You'll warm up. You just have to rub, see?"

"I want my bed." Bonnie's voice wobbled. She was going to cry again. "Maya, can't we get Miss Stewart?"

"We could but this is an island, Bonnie," I said.

We all sat silent. Something dripped at the back of the cave. Bonnie shivered. "We can't phone them," she murmured.

Rose sighed. "No, we can't."

I rubbed Bonnie's cold hands inside the paws of her onesie.

"It isn't an emergency," Bonnie murmured, "is

it?"

I squeezed her hands. "Well…" I reached back in my memory for something. "If it *was* an emergency…"

Bonnie sighed. "So … Miss Stewart said that's what my phone was for. But only if it's an emergency … definitely."

Rose and me stared at each other, our mouths dropping open.

Rose leaped up and discovered Bonnie's sparkly handbag somewhere in the dark behind us. She rummaged around inside it. After a moment she shook her head.

"No, silly, the front pocket," Bonnie said, grabbing it and reaching in. "Ta-da!" She pulled out a chunky pink sparkly phone with pretend jewels all over the case.

"Is it real?" I asked. I pushed the switch on the side. The phone flared into life. There was only a tiny green speck of battery, though. My heart sank. "It's probably useless," I said.

"No, it is *not*. It's my phone," Bonnie said.

"Sorry, yes. And we *are* allowed to use it," I said. "Well done, Bonnie."

Bonnie grinned. "We are *definitely* in an

emergency!"

"I'll ring Dad. *He* won't be so cross with us," I said.

Rose bit her lip.

I tapped in Dad's number.

The phone rang. Then: *I'm not available right now... Please leave your name and number...*

I stopped the call. We looked at each other. "Mum then," Rose said.

"You?" I tried.

"No, you."

I tapped the number. It began to ring. "Hello." Mum's voice, rising strong. "Hello?"

I did a big breath. "Mum, we're on an island and we're stuck and there's Rose and me and Bonnie and it's very cold..."

"Maya! Is that you? You're where? Is this a joke?" Mum's voice turned into a shout, as if she might explode. "Maya, are you all right? Did you say Rose is with you? Put her on. Oh, my God, are you all right?"

I handed the phone to Rose. "It's not a joke," Rose said. "Please listen, Mum."

I put my ear to the phone too. I could hear Mum breathing fast. "Stay where you are. An island.

Oh, my God, I'm ringing Whitesands right now. I'll do it right now!"

The phone cut out. The screen was black. I tried turning it on again, but nothing happened.

"Are they coming?" asked Bonnie.

"Our mum is sorting it out," I said.

"Good," she said and closed her eyes again.

"I'd better switch off the torch again," Rose said, "in case…"

The cave went quiet and much darker, only the sound of the sea roaring outside.

"Do you think Mum understood?" Rose asked. "She will call the teachers, won't she?"

"What time is it?"

"Eight fifteen."

"Mum said to stay where we are, didn't she?" I asked.

Rose shivered. "I'm not going out there. We could fall. It would be worse. We just have to wait."

Home felt so far away. And I thought, just for a moment, at least Rose is with me.

Rose:
Speaking

Nine fifteen. Exactly an hour since we called Mum. I shuffled deeper under the silver blanket and curled against Bonnie. What would they be doing at Whitesands, I wondered, when they realised we were gone? Clemmy wouldn't be able to do the routine on her own. She'd be furious. But then they wouldn't do the Talent Show, would they? They'd search for us. And the teachers would be so angry.

And then, suddenly, out of the dark, Maya said, "You pushed me, Rose."

I listened to the pounding sea outside, understanding straight away.

And I wanted to roar too. "You *told* me to push," I said. "I didn't even want to. You bossed me; you always bossed me."

The cave fell hushed and still. Maya sighed.

I found a big rush of words. "And you think everything's easy for me, but it isn't, cos I don't like Clemmy and I don't want to stay in the squad, so now I haven't got anyone." I scrunched up the edge of the silver foil.

"My leg is going bad. That's why I fell off the pole," Maya said, her voice all small.

"I know."

"No, you didn't," she snapped. "No one knows."

"I knew. I was watching," I said.

"You're always *watching*," Maya said, all angry again.

"Only cos Mum asked me to."

We sat quiet again.

"Do you really not like Clemmy any more?" Maya asked.

"She's horrid to people. She's the one who went to get Miss Bruce. It wasn't me. I told her not to. Anyway, all she wants to do is train."

"I thought you liked training?"

"I do like actual gym. But I'm sick of worrying about it. Clemmy makes me worry. And the coach calls me Rachel. She can't even remember my name." We gathered the silver blanket round our shoulders. "I love drawing and there isn't ever any time," I said.

"You did a good picture of that bottle." Maya paused. "Do you really not want to be in the squad any more?"

"I have to," I said.

"Why, why do you have to?"

"You can't … so I should. You were always really good at gym."

"But if you don't like it?"

The way Maya said that … I started to wonder. "What about Clemmy, though?" I said.

"It's not up to Clemmy. Who cares what she thinks?"

"But Mum…?"

"I could tell Mum … if you want," Maya said. "I could make a joke, so she isn't cross. Anyway, Mum would just be glad if we stopped fighting."

We stared out to sea. Bonnie slept. It was completely night and the sea and sleepiness seemed to drift over us, so we could have been anywhere, anywhere in the whole world.

Maya:
A Real Proper
Adventure

I woke up to the sound of a roar, like a motorbike.

My sister's face was lit up bright by a white light scanning the mouth of our cave.

I wasn't scared. "Wake up," I told Bonnie, tugging at her sleeve.

Rose sprang up, went to the cave mouth and waved the silver blanket, her whole body lit in light.

I put my arm round Bonnie, so she wouldn't be scared. "I think they've come to get us."

The massive bright light lit us all now, like aliens landing, blasting our eyes into the back of our heads. A boat was bouncing on the waves, coming towards us. I couldn't see any people, just black blurs.

Bonnie gripped my hand.

"We're like pirates," I said. "Mr Goodman will have a parrot. *Ooh arr.*"

The lifeboat bounced up on to the sand and we all stepped back because it was so enormous and orange. A man jumped out in a big padded yellow suit, becoming a normal shape and calling out, "Rose, Maya and Bonnie, isn't it? You're going to be fine; we just need to get you all warm."

Bonnie held on to my hand, and I shouted,

"Don't worry. I'm coming too."

The man bellowed, "Are you the one with the injury, love?" over the massive roaring from the engine.

I was going to say no but he had already unrolled a sock-thing for my leg. He padded it with a sort of paddle behind it. "You get to be right at the front," he said. Dad would have said I looked like a cricketer. Then two people carried me on to the lifeboat, a snug blanket was thrown round me and I was in the best place, looking out over the whole sea. The boat sort of reared up like a ride at the fair where you wonder if it might dash away. And off we went, out into the sea, and my heart was racing and water was spattering me in big gusts and it was a proper real adventure. Rose and Bonnie had terrified faces. I wanted to shout "whee!" because it was so fast, and we did huge dips and the land was rising in front of us and I wished the journey could last much longer.

I decided I was going to own a lifeboat one day.

Rose:
A Talk with
Mr Goodman

Mr Goodman ran his hand through his hair. "Now, Rose," he said, "I'm going to let you tell me what happened and then you are going to listen to me. This is a very serious matter."

"It was my idea," I said.

"What? Now, Rose…"

"It was. I knew Maya's leg was getting sore and I said we should go and see the seals on the island one last time to cheer her up. And Bonnie wanted to come too."

Mr Goodman's face was kind. I didn't want to look at that gentle smile. I've always liked Mr Goodman. But he *had* to believe me. He had to. His eyes were very blue, and he was looking at me so hard.

"Rose, what you are telling me really doesn't make sense," he said. "You and Maya don't speak to each other."

"I think we do," I said slowly, "just … not out loud."

Mr Goodman shook his head, smiling.

"It's not Maya's fault about the island. It was a stupid idea, but it was me as well – I didn't have to go. And … we forgot the time… We didn't notice the sea coming over the causeway until it was too late."

He sighed. "Rose, Maya has already told me it was her idea."

"No, it was me. Don't punish Maya… She'll have to go to hospital again… Please, she's … we've… She's my sister."

Mr Goodman rolled his eyes. He threw his hands up in the air. "Bonnie says it was her idea too. That's all three of you! I think I'd better have a chat with all your parents myself."

Maya:
Bonnie's
Bag Again

We weren't exactly heroes, but we were very interesting.

Rose, Bonnie and me all had hot baths in the bath in Mr Goodman's cabin. Teacher towels were bigger and softer than our ones. Mrs Olson checked me and felt my leg all over and asked me lots of questions. "Why didn't you tell us your leg was getting painful?"

"Because I didn't want it," I said. "I wanted it to go away. If you tell someone, it's realer."

She said I had to rest for the last day and go to hospital when I got home. My leg was all bandaged and fat. It wasn't hurting a lot. Now we'd had an adventure everyone wanted to talk to us, and Rose wouldn't say very much so they all asked me.

Bonnie kept telling everyone about the island. "We were waiting for the seals, but we decided they were too smelly."

When I saw Miss Bruce she said, "I'm sorry your leg has been bothering you, Maya. I'll ask Georgie to pack your things for you. For what it's worth I think you have been very brave but also foolish."

"And you have been very bossy," I nearly said,

but didn't.

Dillon came to find me. "Mr Goodman said we're all getting hoodies. He said the parents paid for them as part of the trip."

"I want a purple one with a seal on," I said.

"There weren't very many purple ones," Dillon said. "I saved one for you, though."

Georgie said, "Everyone was rushing around looking for you last night and then the teachers made us search every cabin and nobody even started the Talent Show. And someone said you had caught a bus and gone to Glasgow with all your pocket money from years and years. Miss Stewart cried and said, 'I should have been with Bonnie all the time. I'm really sorry. This is my first School Journey!' And everyone was sent to bed really late after Mr Goodman said you had been found and you were coming home in a lifeboat."

"What if you had got drowned? What if the seals had eaten you? Can't you walk properly again?" Jake asked me.

"We weren't. They didn't. No, I can't," I said. "You would have loved the lifeboat, Jake."

The coach was due to leave in the afternoon, so we watched bits of the Talent Show all morning.

I liked the magic best. Rose and Clemmy did their gymnastics routine and lots of people sang things. Pip's dance group had been practising for ages and made everyone copy their steps. Georgie was packing the cabin and I was sitting outside when Bonnie rushed out to find me. She held out her pink handbag and said, "I've got it!"

"What have you got?" I said. "If it's shells, you should just pick the best ones, Bonnie. I'll help you, if you want."

"No," she said, her face all lit up. "It's not shells. I've found HIM."

"Found who?"

"Look!" She opened the bag. There, on top of the notebooks and flower press and hat and phone, scrabbling to climb up the lining of the bag, was a small brown furry animal. Nibble. "He was back in the bathroom where we left him," Bonnie said.

"Wow, Bonnie. You're brilliant. I'll tell Archie… No, you can tell him."

So she did.

Archie looked as if he might burst. "He must have gone for a walk and come back. What did he find to eat, though?" he said.

"Oh, stop worrying. He's back. Give him some food and some water," I said.

"I can't believe it!" Archie hugged Bonnie, then me. "I can't believe he's coming home!"

Rose:
Being the
Best I Can Be

We waited to do our routine behind a screen in the cafeteria. Clemmy was odd and quiet. When Dillon was doing his stand-up comedy just before our turn, Clemmy said, "We're not prepared enough, Rose."

"No, we aren't," I said.

"We won't be the best we can be," she said.

"No, we won't," I said. There didn't seem to be anything else to say.

"Is it true you saved the others from a seal attack?" Clemmy asked.

"Yes," I said.

"That's actually quite cool. Did the seal…"

"I don't want to be in the squad any more." There. I'd said it. And Maya wasn't even there to help me.

Clemmy fixed me with a strong stare. "I know I said you were borderline, Rose, but…"

"I don't like training, Clemmy." I said. "I think being the best I can be might mean not doing so much gym."

"Oh!"

She went into a squat. I copied.

"Might you just come and do gym sometimes?" she asked.

"Yes," I said. "Yes, I will."

Miss Stewart must have been feeling better because she said well done to lots of people when they came off stage. Mr Goodman played the guitar really well. He sang a song he wrote for his wife who had just had a baby. "Has anyone else got something they want to show the rest of us?" he asked. "Who hasn't shared something? It could be a thing you collected, like Bonnie's shells or something you do. Or you could just tell us about something. Has anyone not had a chance?"

We looked round the group.

"Maya hasn't done anything?" Bonnie said. "She should tell a story."

"My sister's really good at stories," I said.

Everyone turned to look at me.

"No, I'm not," Maya said.

"Yes, you are," I said. "You've always been good at telling stories and when we were … quite worried … on the island, you told a story to me and Bonnie. To both of us."

So she started. But this was a new story.

"Once there was a seal and a butterfly. The butterfly spent her days flying around and everyone watched her because she was elegant. And the seal, who was her friend, spent her days in the sea because when she swam she was like a piece of the sea, all twisting and coiling. She had her own island.

"Anyway, one evening, there was a huge storm with lashing waves and pounding thunder and a boat with some people in it got stranded on the rocks. *Bash bash*.

"'Oh no,' they all cried, 'we are going to perish.' No one could help the poor passengers who were on a school trip and very frightened. 'Help, help! If this boat turns over, we will drown, and all our families will be so sad.' But no one could hear them because the storm was too loud. But there was someone who could understand the danger and that was the seal, and she called to the butterfly, 'Come on!'

"The seal swam through the lashing waves and the butterfly flew through the pounding thunder and when they got to the boat the seal went round and round it and pushed it off the rocks with her head. She harnessed her neck in the ropes at the front and the butterfly flew high and looked for which way to go, then came down to land on the seal's nose to keep her going in the right direction. 'Go that way. Just keep going straight,' she told her. 'I won't leave you!' And they zoomed over the sea, up on a wave and down the other side, frothing and foaming everywhere around them, and the strong seal pulling and pulling.

"After a lot of dragging they were back at the beach, so all the passengers climbed out of the boat and they clapped and cried, and the seal and the butterfly bowed. Well, the seal bowed her long neck and the butterfly bent her elegant body. 'You are a Lifeboat Rescue Service!' called a passenger. 'Congratulations to the Seal and Butterfly Lifeboat Rescue Service. Hooray!'"

We all clapped. The teachers were clapping as well.

Maya:
Welcome
Home Again

Two things happened. Well, more than two, but two main ones. Rose and me got off the coach together because, actually, we had been sitting together all the way back, even though Bonnie played games with us the whole way, so I suppose we were a three really. But we did get off the coach together, and Mum and Gran were both there to meet us, and Mum hugged both of us at the same time.

I said, "Rose doesn't want to compete any more in gym because she's sick of it."

And Rose said, "Maya should do the drama club in May because Miss Stewart says we can use her stories to make the drama club play."

And Gran said, "Don't we get a word in edgeways? What's this I hear about you two wandering off in the night and getting yourselves in trouble?"

And Mum just hugged and hugged and hugged us and I realised she hadn't said anything ... not one single thing, except "welcome home".

Rose:
Archie's
Surprise

And it was so funny that when Archie got home his mum said, "Come and see Nibble Two." All his family pretended they had been looking after Nibble when they had obviously got a new hamster, so now Archie has two hamsters, but he's going to give the new one to Bonnie to thank her. And I'm writing this in Maya's bedroom, because I like being in Maya's bedroom. The doctor says Maya won't need a big operation, just an adjustment of her pins.

Maya

And I said, "I have to be better by May."

And the doctor said, "Have you got something planned?"

"I'm making a play," I said.

Rose

And I'm making the set, with Gran helping.

Maya

It's a beach with rocks and the sea. And seals.

Rose

It won't smell like seals, though.

Maya and Rose

Because seals smell terrible.

Acknowledgements

The story of Maya and Rose is very much rooted in school life and friendships. A School Journey is a powerful experience for children. They come back changed and enriched by this time away from home. The pupils I have worked with in Fern Hill and Malden Manor schools in Kingston upon Thames continue to inspire me in many ways.

As a parent of three children, I've obviously thought a lot about sibling relationships and watched them spark before my eyes!

As ever, big thanks to:

My family, who support and encourage me on good days and more difficult ones: The Howes: Adrian, Miranda, Ella and Judith and The Briggses: D and D, Al and Nancy.

Anne Clark, my agent, for her excellent help and advice.

Tom Bonnick, my editor who helped me to focus on the emotional heart of this story, and all the staff at Nosy Crow.

My writers' group (Julian, Kryss, Lesley, Carolyn, and Clare) who meet regularly at the National

Theatre in London. Thanks for honest feedback and all your ideas.

Sue Wallman, Sue Durrant, Jess Palmer, Alison Allen and Yvonne Hennessy: Thanks for your friendship and inspiration.